# SATISFY ME

# SATISFY ME

## A collection of twenty erotic stories

### Edited by Miranda Forbes

Published by Accent Press Ltd – 2008
ISBN 9781906125882

Printed and bound in the UK



Cover Design by
Red Dot Design

# Contents

# Victoria Learns Discipline
## by Angela Meadows

The oil lamp gave me a ghostly appearance in the long mirror due to my white-stockinged legs, white satin bloomers and corset, and the white skin of my face and exposed breasts. The only contrast was my brown hair and my small red nipples.

For the first time since I had arrived at the Venus School for Young Ladies some six weeks earlier, I stood in the study of Madame Thackeray, the Principal. Why I was there I wasn't sure. Somehow I had displeased her while pleasuring young Albert during the evening's lesson. Now I stood patiently awaiting her, standing beside her desk and looking at my image. To my right was a large bed, as this was Madame's bedroom as well her office. The bed had heavy wooden head- and foot-boards with pineapple-shaped knobs at each corner. At the foot of the bed was a strange, waist-high stool. It was in the form of an elephant standing on four sturdy legs. Its trunk and two curved tusks pressed against the bed and it had a broad, padded leather back.

I turned my gaze to Madame's desk. It bore just four items, two of which were framed photographs. One showed two ladies which I recognised in the dim light as being Madame Thackeray herself and Madame Hulot, her companion and assistant. They were dressed in light blouses and dark skirts and carried parasols. The other photo was a different style entirely as it showed a naked woman facing the photographer with a fine scarf suspended lazily from her right hand. She appeared to have no body hair whatsoever. I peered closely and was a little astonished to confirm that the figure was Madame Hulot.

The other two items on the desk also seemed rather incongruous for that of a school principal. One was a black leather riding crop and the other was a magnificent ebony phallus. I bent to look at the latter more closely. It was broader and longer than the glass instruments that Madame had given us to practise with, and it had a pair of fist-sized testicles at one end. The other end was a helmet-shaped knob so large that I thought I would barely be able to get my hand around it. I could not imagine what use such a tool could be put to, but further examination was prevented by the scrape of the door opening. I stood up straight.

Madame swept in, circled me and sat at the chair behind her desk. Although surely in her early forties she was a handsome woman with long fair hair piled up on her head. She rested her hands on the leather desktop and looked up at me.

"What is your purpose here, Victoria," she asked curtly.

"To study the arts and sciences required to manage our future husband's household and affairs and to satisfy him in any way that he desires," I recited the oft-heard catechism of Madame Thackeray's school.

"That is correct, Victoria, but you disappoint me. You have shown great aptitude for the arts of love but it seems that you cannot resist taking pleasure yourself."

2

"But, Madame," I protested, "You taught us to find pleasure in being touched and how to arouse excitement in our private parts."

"I did indeed and valuable lessons they are, but what you have not yet learned is that there is a time to indulge your own pleasure and a time to devote to servicing your lover. Caressing and coaxing the male member requires all your attention, not least in preventing him from reaching a climax too soon. Instead of using both hands on your man you had one hand up your fanny."

"I am sorry, Madame."

"You will be, Victoria. However there is another matter and that concerns Albert. He has a marvellous attribute and will be a great asset to us here, but he is inexperienced and spurts far too readily. As well as learning your own lesson you must teach him restraint." I was nonplussed; what did Madame mean? She answered my unspoken question immediately.

"You will spend an hour each day before supper, handling Albert's magnificent cock. You will ensure he retains his erection for the whole hour without ejaculating and you will refrain from fingering yourself in that time. A senior girl will observe and record transgressions. Next Sunday you will report to me at three of the clock and we will examine your progress. Each failure will be rewarded with a stroke of this." Madame raised the crop and brandished it at me, "And now I will give you a taste of what to expect if you fail."

My heart beat faster as I realised that she intended to beat me.

"Remove your bloomers if you please, Victoria." I had little choice but to obey Madame. I tugged on the ribbon at my waist. The bow undid and the garment duly dropped to the floor. I stepped out of it.

"Now bend over the elephant." The purpose of the strange stool had become apparent. I stepped slowly and fearfully towards it. When my thighs rested against the cool leather, Madame pushed against the small of my back with the riding crop. I bent forward until my stomach was resting on the padded back of the elephant. My arms and my hair dangled down.

"Further," Madame urged. I raised myself up on the tip of my toes and found myself delicately balanced on the elephant's back. I felt Madame's slippered foot slide between my ankles and push my legs apart. My feet lost contact with the floor and I really was lying across the stool. I was very conscious that my buttocks were as exposed as they could be, as were my most private parts. I lay there listening to Madame's soft breaths as some moments passed. Not even my dear, strict father had beaten me before so I had no idea what to expect. I trembled in anticipation. There was a fizz through the air and my left buttock burst into flame. I yelped, but before I could take a breath there came another screech of the crop and my right buttock exploded.

"Please, Madame," I appealed, but to no avail as the crop scorched across my left cheek a second time. I tried to struggle off the stool.

"Be still, Victoria," She was breathing deeply now, but her energy was not expended as the crop came down again on my right buttock. I screamed out, as it felt that both my cheeks were aflame.

"That is enough for now," Madame said soothingly. I remained thrown over the whipping stool like a sack of potatoes over a donkey. I sobbed but the pain began to subside a little.

I felt a pressure in the small of my back, a finger that began to slide between my cheeks. It lingered, circling

4

around my arsehole. Despite the smouldering fire in my buttocks the touch was like an electric shock. It became the centre of my attention. The finger moved on, parting my lips and slipping inside. I realised that my juices were flowing. The finger delved deeper and was joined by its neighbours and by a thumb that felt for and found my swelling button. I groaned as the pleasure competed with the pain of the beating. In fact the pleasure seemed greater than I had ever experienced. In a few moments I was moaning as pulses of indescribable desire rippled through my abdomen. My thighs shook uncontrollably and I came with a gasp and cry. The hand withdrew.

"There, that will teach you something, Victoria. Pain and pleasure complement each other, the former raising the latter to a new plane of sensation. You may dismount now."

A little wriggling shifted my weight so that I slid off the elephant and onto my unsteady legs. I turned to face Madame. She was standing holding the door open, my bloomers dangling from an outstretched finger.

"Don't forget – five of the clock each evening, in the drawing room. Return to your room now." I grabbed the under-garment and fled from the room and up the stairs.

When I reached my bedroom I flung myself face down on the bed. My bottom still burned but my thoughts were of the ecstasy that Madame had given me. Barely a few moments passed before there was a knock on the door, and a whispered voice asked, "Victoria, are you there?" I recognised the French accent of my friend, Natalie.

"Come in," I called, my voice breaking somewhat. The door opened.

"Oh, Victoria, what has happened to you?" Natalie approached me and I could see her wide eyes staring at my bottom. "Has Madame beaten you? You have a cross of red marks on your smooth, white bottom." I explained what Madame had said and the punishment I had received. Natalie laid her hand gently on my bottom.

"Ooh, I can feel the heat still," Then I began to describe how Madame had caressed me.

"Do you mean like this," Natalie's finger traced out the same path as Madame's and again my loins trembled with the delectable pleasure.

"Yes, just like that," I moaned. Natalie pressed her hand between my swollen lips.

"You are indeed excited, Victoria. I am sure that just a little movement like this," her fingers rubbed in and out of my vagina, "will make you come."

"I … I think you are correct," I gasped as the tremulations increased to a climax.

Afterwards we lay together on the bed and discussed the strange way that the beating I had been given seemed to make me quicker to achieve orgasm.

"Perhaps, Madame will find occasion to use her whip, on me," said Natalie almost wistfully.

As the clock in the hallway struck five, I entered the drawing room. My room-mate, Beatrice, one year my senior, was sitting on a couch, sewing in the light of the sun that was about to set beyond the mountain peaks. As I stepped towards her I heard footsteps behind me and turned to see Albert joining us. Bea put down her work and looked at each of us.

"Good afternoon Albert," Albert nodded his head in greeting, "Hello, Victoria. You know what you have to do." I turned to face Albert and pressed a hand against his groin. His cock was already hard and straining at his lederhosen.

"You are not going to do it in those clothes are you, Victoria?" Bea's voice carried a note of authority. I looked down at my long grey woollen skirt and high-necked, long-sleeved, white linen blouse, "You do not want to get semen on your day uniform. Take it off." I had no argument to put to Bea, so unbuttoned my blouse and slipped it off my shoulders, then unfastened my skirt and let it drop to the floor. I stepped out of it and stood somewhat self-consciously in my slip.

"And the rest," I looked at Bea questioningly, "Yes, I said take off your slip. Don't waste time." Bea seemed to enjoy giving me orders. I grasped the hem of my slip and pulled it up over my head. For the first time in my life I stood unclothed in front of a man, well a boy, as that was all that Albert was really. His eyes widened as he took in the full sight of my naked body. His adoring look immediately excited me and I felt my nipples swell and perk up. I began to sway from side to side feeling extremely sensuous. My breasts swung in response to my movement and Albert's head followed them.

"Now release him, and get down to work," I came to my senses and remembered what I was supposed to be doing. I knelt in front of Albert and undid the buttons of his flies. Before I had finished his erect penis pushed through the suede leather and throbbed a few inches from my face. He pushed the braces from his shoulders and the shorts slid down his legs. He pulled his smock over his head and then stood naked but for his knee-length woollen socks and the slippers that the men wore inside the house. The rays of the sunset streamed through the window and illuminated his body. His skin seemed to give off a golden glow. I gazed at his marvellous tool, so long, so broad, so firm. There was a tingling between my legs and I lowered my arm so that my hand could find its way between my thighs. My fingers found my crack.

"Victoria, I can see what you are doing. That's one black mark against you." Bea's sharp words wakened me as if from a dream. I remembered Madame's command that I must not pleasure myself but concentrate on Albert. I resolved to do as I was told.

I placed my right hand under Albert's testicles and felt their weight on my palm. I caressed his scrotum with my fingers, the coarse curly hairs like a nest. I encircled my left hand around his shaft, my fingertips just meeting my thumb. I pushed my hand away from me pulling back his foreskin. His shiny, purple knob appeared and the tiny hole in the tip gaped. Albert moaned. I looked up to see that he had thrown his head back and he had clenched his fists either side of his thighs.

I closed my right hand around his balls and pulled my left hand towards me. The glans disappeared in the folds of the foreskin. I repeated the movement just once but that was enough. Albert moaned again and shuddered and thick white semen gushed out of the penis and covered my bosom. It dribbled down between my two breasts. I released Albert's penis and testicles from my grip.

"That's hardly a good start, Victoria," Bea's sneer indicated her low opinion of my skills, "it hasn't been five minutes yet. You've got to hold him at the edge for an hour. You had better start again."

Albert had sunk to the floor and was lying stretched out on his back on the thick carpet. His penis, though still three or four inches in length, flopped flaccidly against a thigh.

"What should I do?" I appealed to Bea.

"Caress him, his whole body, not just his cock. Use your bosom."

I knelt beside Albert and allowed my fingers to

8

wander over his smooth hairless chest. He murmured with satisfaction. I lowered myself further until my nipples touched his skin then I moved from side to side so that my breasts made random curved patterns over his abdomen. The movement gave me pleasure too and my nipples become as hard as acorns. Albert opened his eyes and stared at me with a look of utter amazement. I glanced at his groin and saw his penis stir. I continued to move but watched in fascination as his cock unfolded and grew. It rose higher and higher straining towards the ceiling. The purple head forced its way through the foreskin and emerged like the fruit of some tropical plant. I was surprised by the light touch of fingers on my breasts. I looked round and saw Albert's hands cupping and caressing my pendulous bosom. The touch sent a thrill to my stomach and beyond. I could feel my lips swelling and parting. I was in a dreamy state of pleasure and unable to think as my hand slipped between the folds of my vulva.

"Victoria! That's twice." I withdrew my hand and awoke with a start. I knew that Bea would report my misdemeanours to Madame Thackeray and my buttocks tingled with the anticipation of another beating.

Albert continued to massage my breasts while I leaned over him. He was stretching his legs and pointing his toes. I reached out my right hand to grasp his erect tool, but as I did he was convulsed with a spasm and another glob of semen spurted from the hole.

"Well, I suppose that was a bit better. At least he lasted fifteen minutes that time." Bea sighed, "You still have forty minutes left, Victoria."

It took a little longer to revive Albert after his second ejaculation but allowing him to play with my breasts and nipples kept his attention. I ran my hands all over his young, taut limbs and trunk, exploring a man's body for the first time. It was so much firmer than a female's, the muscles hard beneath the silky skin. He explored my body too, his long, supple fingers tracing the marks of the crop on my buttocks. His long, eager cock trembled and waved as we embraced and moved over each other but I succeeded in restraining him from another orgasm. My resolve only slipped as the clock struck six. He was kneeling over me and I reached between his legs to grasp his tool with both hands. Albert groaned and arched his back. White drops of semen dripped on to my stomach.

"Your time is up, Victoria. You can dress now Albert." Albert stood up and pulled on his lederhosen while I lay back exhausted.

The next day at the same time, Albert and I met again in the drawing room. We undressed and got to work caressing each other. Today it was Helga who was supervising us and waiting for me to make a mistake. Helga was a big, fair German girl whose conversation seemed to consist of shouted commands. Albert and I had been busy for about twenty minutes without mishap when my hand slipped between my legs. Helga was vigilant.

"Nein, Victoria. You must not," she bawled. Albert paused in his manipulation of my breasts and spoke to Helga in German. They proceeded to have a conversation. At last he turned to me and smiled broadly.

"I have explained your task to Albert," Helga explained loudly, "He now understands that you are not allowed to play with your own private parts but he asks if there is any reason why he should not touch you there." Helga shrugged, "If he wishes to do so I see no reason why he should not."

Albert reached out, took my hand and guided me to the couch. He beckoned for me to sit down. When I had done so he knelt at my feet. I lay back and he pushed my knees apart and gazed adoringly at the wonders that I kept between my legs. I could not see much of what was happening from my reclining position but I imagined that his penis was still firm and wobbling gently. Albert placed his hand on the softest skin at the top of my thigh and wound the short curly hairs around his forefinger. Then he used both hands to peel my lips apart. He lowered his head until his hair and ears touched the skin of my legs. I was waiting for something but I was not sure what was to come. The muscles in my buttocks were tense and my fanny throbbed. When the touch finally came I let out a gasp. His tongue touched my clitoris then slid down into my crack. Warmer and softer than a finger, the feeling was exquisite. He lapped at my hole which I knew was oozing my juices. He had started slowly but steadily he increased the speed of the rhythmic movement. I knew that I was trying to teach Albert restraint but I could not stop myself from being carried away on the wave of orgasm. I sighed and arched my back as the pleasure took me. He sucked greedily on my fanny gripping my buttocks in his strong hands then gently allowed me to subside panting on to the couch.

Albert stood up and I was delighted to see his penis still proudly erect. I slid from the couch onto my knees in front of him and eagerly caressed the magnificent tool. I took care not to grip it to hard but touched and flicked my fingers up and down the shaft, under and around his balls and the crack between his cheeks. I was torn between wanting to give him satisfaction and achieving my task. I am afraid to say that the former won and in a few moments he too shuddered and a fountain of white foam spurted over me. Albert laughed.

"We start again," he said while Helga harrumphed in the background.

The next day, Friday, we again had just one accidental orgasm and on the Saturday we reached the chimes for six of the clock with not even one. Bea was again watching over us and had shown considerable interest in Albert's eager exploration of my bosom and fanny. Now I was ever so carefully caressing Albert's erect member and touching the tip gently with my fingertips. At the end of the hour he was begging to be allowed to come and his penis almost trembled with impatience. As the hall clock struck six Bea left her seat and came towards us.

"Well done Victoria, you can stop now."

She pushed me gently but firmly to the side and knelt in front of Albert. She opened her mouth and lent forward so that her lips surrounded the glowing head of Albert's penis. Albert groaned as his knob disappeared into Bea's mouth. Although I considered Albert's penis to be exceptionally long and thick, still Bea inched forward taking more and more of it down her throat. Albert staggered and steadied himself by placing his hands on her head. His hips jerked as if to thrust his manhood further into her. I could not believe it when her nose finally rubbed against his pubic hair. Almost immediately Albert shuddered and his hips vibrated rapidly. I thought Bea would choke but she held onto his thighs while he shot his load straight down her gullet. Moments later he edged backwards, and his penis emerged shrunken and wrinkled. Bea gasped and took quick, deep breaths. She licked her lips and looked at me triumphantly.

"There, that's how you avoid getting semen on your

clothes." She laughed while I still looked at her in wonderment.

"How do you do that? How can you swallow a huge cock and not gag?"

"I don't know, Victoria. It's just something I can do. I know that very few girls can do it even if they have tried. But the boys like it." I looked at Albert still standing and swaying slightly with a blissful expression on his face. I began to pull my slip over my head.

"Tomorrow I have to face Madame," I said sadly.

"Do not worry, Victoria," Bea replied kindly, "while you had some misadventures earlier you have shown today that you can keep Albert excited for an hour without allowing him to reach orgasm. That is a very great skill. I am sure you have already discovered that though Madame sticks to her word, she likes to mix rewards with punishment." She gave me one of her knowing smiles and I wondered if she too had been disciplined by Madame Thackeray. I looked forward to the next day with curiosity as well as apprehension.

# Booby Call
## by Landon Dixon

I work for one of the big cola companies, collecting change and stocking vending machines on a route that takes me from high-rise office buildings to low-track motels. I see a lot of bubbly babes during the course of my carbonated travels, and, like a ship's captain, I have a special girl in every port of call – a couple of whom I'm actually banging as regularly as the shutter door on my truck.

One of the girls is Lola, a busty secretary at a suburban high school. She's built the way a woman should be built – from the tits out – with huge knockers that she's not the least bit shy about showing off, in high-tension tank tops and stitch-straining sweaters. She has long, jet-black hair and flashing green eyes to go along with the blazing headlights, and a slim, spicy body sporting an overstuffed rear-end almost as impressive as her all-natural front bumpers.

Lola's the Thursday eleven o'clock stop on my route, and she makes even going back to school fun. Like the sweltering day a couple of weeks ago when the chesty Latina was wearing nothing more than a sleeveless satin blouse, a black leather miniskirt, and a pair of red pumps. She was explicitly violating at least ten articles of the school's dress code, and the laws of distraction, but none of the students or staff at the all-boys educational establishment were complaining.

"Hi, Lola," I exhaled, ogling the voluptuous vixen standing at the front counter, as I wheeled my dolly-full of drinks into the office.

"Oh, hi, Jeff," she casually responded. She gave me a little smile and wink when I ran over the clown-like feet of a gangly kid parked outside the Principal's office.

The kid hardly noticed, what with the gravity of Lola's boobs in the room, attracting all the attention. I pushed past him and strolled down the hall that led to the teachers' lounge, my head swelling with what I knew was to come, and with whom. There were a couple of teachers lounging around next to the drink machine, bitching about their wives and boasting about their school secretary. I quickly unlocked the machine and unloaded my canned and bottled goods, making as much noise as possible.

After I'd done my duty, stocked the machine and sent the horny, horn-rimmed academics packing, my flared nostrils suddenly detected a new scent in the cologne-heavy room – the soft, sweet smell of Lola's perfume. I spun around on my heels and there she was, staring at me, her eyes and heavy-calibre guns locked on-target.

"Jeff," she said coyly, hooking a slender, brown finger in between her glossy lips. "I hate to ask, but can you get a box of paper out of the supply room for me? It's way too heavy for me to carry, and since you've got … the right equipment and all …"

I nodded, eyeing the top-heavy chica and grinning like a kid who's just been awarded a D double-plus. "Sure," I replied, for the benefit of anyone listening to our cover story. "Be glad to."

I followed the girl's twitching butt cheeks and gleaming legs out of the teachers' lounge and back up the hallway. They took a sharp left and we were in the room that housed a humungous photocopier, and beyond that, the locked supply room. Lola lifted the silver chain around her neck and pulled a brass key out of her plunging cleavage, and then bent over slightly and unlocked the door.

I parked my lift-dolly as my live dolly flicked on the lights in the supply room. She turned halfway around and beckoned me inside. Her twin peaks were in stunning profile, and I licked parched lips and swallowed hard and dry. Then I hustled into the supply room after her, my prick as rigid as a yardstick.

I shut the door and pushed in the lock and grabbed the boys' school fantasy in my arms, mashing my mouth against hers. She moaned, grabbed on to my head, knocking my cap flying and clutching at my hair as I clutched her. We kissed ferociously, then frenched like we were in Mr Larouche's language class. Lola's round mounds pressed against my chest, her thick tongue squirming around inside my mouth, her tits and tongue knocking the wind right out of me.

"God, I've been waiting to do this all week!" she gasped, echoing my thoughts exactly. Then she caught my slippery sticker between her dazzling white teeth and started sucking on it, blowing tongue like I well knew she could blow cock.

I grunted my satisfaction and gripped her bum, sliding my sweaty hands up and under her dangerously short skirt and going skin-on-skin with her firm, plump butt cheeks. It was pantyless Thursday, as usual, and I roughly kneaded her sassy seat cushions, lifting the hot-blooded and bodied babe clear off the ground, as she anxiously sucked on my tongue.

"Let's see your tits!" I hissed, when she'd finally given me back my talking-tool.

She glanced up at me and smiled wickedly, her chest heaving and her eyes ablaze. Then she shoved me back and popped the buttons on her blouse open. She spun around, shimmied the shiny garment off her buff, brown shoulders, teasing me. The stretched-out top fluttered to the floor, joining my tongue there, as Lola toyed with the twenty-pound-test hooks that barely held her satiny, pink bra together at the back.

"Fuck that!" I growled, grabbing the titted tart's hot little hands and flinging them aside. I unhooked her chest protector with the agile fingers of the unabashed tit-man – a man who'd worshipped overblown boobs ever since the sweaty, pimply days of Victoria Principal's double-barrelled exploits on *Dallas*, and Dolly Parton's bust-out movie role in *Nine to Five*; and the sleepless, pillow-humping nights of Elvira, Mistress of the Dark's, hey-day.

Lola turned around to face me, arms squeezed together to keep her deep-cupped bra in place, exhibiting enough yawning cleavage to make even the Grand Canyon envious. "These what you're after?' she giggled, dropping her arms to her sides, and her bra to the floor.

Her ta-tas hung huge and heavy right in front of me, golden-brown globes pressure-capped by protruding, caramel-coated nipples. Twin silver rings hung from her pierced jutters, and tattooed across the tops of her titanic tits, in gothic script, were the words 'Handle with Care'. She was a wild child, all right, and she cried out with joy when I grabbed onto her jugs and squeezed.

"Feel up my titties!" she yelped, the photocopier whirring, pumping out paper, in the room next door.

17

I steered the breast-blessed babe further into the supply room, till her bum bumped into a wooden desk that stood against the back wall. Then I hefted her boobs and bent my head down and licked at her nipples.

"Mmmm!" she groaned, closing her eyes and biting her lip.

I knew from our previous sessions just how super-sensitive the hottie's hooters were, so I swirled my tongue all around first one stiff, rubbery nipple and then the other, tonguing them even longer and harder, my hands mauling her massive mams as I did so. Then I latched my lips onto one of her nipples and sucked on it, tugged on it, pulled on her ring, nursing tit like I expected a warm gush of nourishment any second.

"Suck my titties!" Lola wailed. She lifted her arms and ran her fingers through her shimmering, night-shaded tresses, thrusting out and abandoning her treasure chest to my loving hands and mouth.

I sucked long and hard on her one tit, scouring the underside of it with my thrashing tongue, biting into its swollen nipple. Then repeated the erotic process with her other burgeoning boob. Before shoving her jugs together and slashing my tongue back and forth across both of the babe's wickedly flared nipples at once.

Lola's body and boobs shuddered in my hands, but I kept right on with the tongue-lashing, desperately feeling up her smooth, superheated tit-flesh. Until at last her eyes popped open and she hissed, "Fuck me!"

I unhanded her damp breasts in order that she could unhook her skirt, so that I could unbuckle and unzip my pants, and drop them and my drawers. Lola jumped ass-backwards onto the desk and spread her legs, her shaven snatch winking with wetness. I shuffled forward, in between her slim, honey-dipped limbs, my arrow-straight cock pointing stiffly and directly at the girl's slit, straining to find a home there.

"Fuck me!" she urged, leaning back against the wall and gathering up her splayed breasts and squeezing them.

I shouldered her legs, gulped down some air, and then parted her slick pussy lips with my mushroomed cocktop. I pushed forward, diving deep into the luscious lady's sopping twat. I started pumping my hips, slowly at first, then faster and faster, getting a good, hard fucking rhythm going. I churned my rod back and forth in Lola's tight, juicy cunt, the desk banging into the wall, my girl's ass and boobs shivering with each and every cock-thrust.

"Gimme those tits!" I yelled, brushing her hands away and grabbing onto her brown jugs. I groped them, rolled and pulled nipples, relentlessly pistoning my pulsating cock in and out of her pussy.

She gripped the edge of the scraping desk with white-knuckled fingers and desperately twisted her head back and forth against the wall, raven locks falling over and sticking to her perspiration-slick face. "I'm coming!" she screamed.

I shifted it into fifth gear, fucking the hootered honey in a frenzy, my lower body smacking against her rippling butt cheeks, my battering-ram cock splitting her in two. "I'm coming, too, baby!" I gritted.

Her body jerked and her jugs jounced around in my greasy hands, as I hammered the both of us headlong into orgasm. The sperm in my balls boiled out-of-control and shot up my shaft and spray-painted the velvet walls of the girl's gushing pussy. I blasted wad after white-hot wad into Lola's love tunnel, in time to the electric shocks jolting our bodies.

When it was finally all over, I exhaustedly toyed with the girl's glistening melons, gently squeezing them, primping her nipples, as she quivered with the afterquakes of ecstasy. As my still-hard cock sluiced slowly back and forth in her dripping slit. "Same time next week, baby?" I said.

Her emerald eyes opened up and met mine. "I'm the only one, right, lover?" she asked. "'Cause I don't share with anyone else."

"S-sure, of course," I mumbled. But my fuzzy mind was already flashing forward to the late-afternoon stop on my route – at the hospital, where redheaded, big-breasted Nurse Mary awaited me, thirsty for the taste of cola and cock.

Everything went according to schedule that week: Lola in the morning, Mary in the afternoon. I delivered the fizzy goods with a song in my heart, a smile on my face, and a spring in my step, and prick. But the following Thursday, when I made my regular stop at St. John's Memorial after a scorching pre-lunch eat-me session with Lola, my tit-bliss worlds collided in a most disturbing fashion.

I was bang on time at 3:45, and by four o'clock I had the machines in the hospital cafeteria locked and loaded and ready to spew fluids, like me. I trucked on down the hallway, took a flight of stairs leading to the basement two steps at a time, and then slipped into the laundry room. It wasn't exactly the most romantic place in the world, but on-the-job lovers can't be choosers. At that time of day the room was unoccupied, leaving me and Mary plenty of time and space to get thoroughly fluffed and folded.

I strode past the industrial-sized washers and dryers, the tangy scent of laundry detergent filling my nose, until I came to the linen storage closet. I cracked the door open and poked my head inside, a gleam in my eye and steel in my dick. Only, I didn't just see lovely, top-heavy Mary waiting for me; I saw Mary and Lola waiting for me! In each other's arms!

Lola said, "Hi, Jeff," as I stumbled inside and shut the door.

"H-hi, Lola ... Mary," I responded vaguely. The shock of Lola discovering my afternoon delight, and obviously making it her own, shunted the shit-eating grin off my face and unhinged my jaw.

The two chesty chicks were bumper-to-bumper, naked from the neck down, their bodies a study in stunning contrast (except in two important areas, of course). Mary's the exact opposite of Lola, in personality and distinguishing features. She has big blue eyes, short red hair, and a pale, delicately-featured face. And the sight of her plump, porcelain figure jammed up against Lola's lusty bronze bod was mind-bending, to say the least. The prominent physical traits the two girls shared were their breasts, Mary's every bit as big as Lola's – round and firm and lightly shot through with little blue veins, her incher nipples obscenely pink against their ivory backgrounds.

"I followed you here last week, Jeff," Lola explained. "Found out you were cheating on me." She turned her head and kissed Mary on the mouth. Mary blushed, but she didn't take her pale, petite hands off Lola's brazen butt cheeks. "I told you I don't share my lovers with anyone else."

Lola slid her fingers into Mary's hair and jerked the girl's head forward, pressing her lips against Mary's lipstick-smeared mouth. They kissed deeply, devouring each other's mouths, their hot, breasty bodies glued together in glorious nudity. I stood there and gaped, unsure if the two babes were actually serious about each

21

other or just putting on a show for me.

Lola answered both my questions by pulling her mouth away from Mary and saying, "Enjoy this farewell, Jeff. 'Cause from here on in Mary and I are lovers – exclusively. Right, girlfriend?"

Mary gazed dazedly at Lola's glossy lips, as if trying to figure out what they'd just said. Then she nodded her head and stuck out her kitten-pink tongue and licked Lola's lips, securing the Latina's sweet revenge.

I groaned, having just gone from two busty, bang-away broads to none. But at least they were giving me something to remember them by. So I unzipped my pants, pulled out my cock, and started stroking.

Lola and Mary frenched one another, their tongues tumbling together over and over, Lola clawing at Mary's hair, Mary clenching Lola's butt, me fisting my dick. Then Lola broke tongue-contact with the flame-haired beauty and pushed back a little. She grasped Mary's enormous boobs and began fondling them.

"Yes, feel up my breasts!" Mary bleated, tilting her head back.

"Yeah, feel up her tits!" I growled, buffing my dong.

Lola caressed Mary's bowling ball-sized hooters, tracing fire all over their vast, sensitive surfaces with her fingernails, tweaking the girl's engorged nipples with her thumbs.

Mary groaned, her body trembling. "Suck my tits!" she cried, putting into startling words what I'd been thinking and praying for.

Lola lifted Mary's left breast and teased its extended nip with the tip of her saucy tongue. She licked at the underside of Mary's nipple, then swirled her tongue all over and around the gasping girl's pebbly, pink areola. Before vacuuming the inflamed protuberance into her mouth and sucking on it.

I cranked my pole-polishing up another ten notches, as Lola tugged on my former lover's tits, her hands clasping and kneading Mary's knockers. The redhead's dewy body shivered with delight. Until she eventually shook off Lola's mouth and hands and laid down some sensuous tit-play of her own, doing to the Spanish hottie's ta-tas what Lola had done to hers.

"Yeah, baby!" Lola breathed, Mary juggling the girl's burnished breasts, licking and sucking and biting into her mocha buds, yanking on her nipple rings.

My sweet, innocent Mary was anything but sweet and innocent just then, chewing hungrily on her lover's meaty nipples and queen-sized tits in a lesbian frenzy. She pushed Lola's boobs apart and excitedly lapped at the girl's golden cleavage. As I furiously jacked my rock-hard dick, my nut sack tightening in ominous anticipation, the temperature in the stuffy room spiking a hundred degrees.

"Finger-fuck me!" Lola suddenly screamed.

Mary left one of her hands on Lola's breasts while she dove the other down to the firecracker's pussy. She slid two purple-tipped fingers into Lola's baby-faced slit, started pumping. Lola gasped, shuddered. Then she got a good grip on one of Mary's mams and plugged her own silver-ringed digits into her lover's fur-dappled sex.

"Holy shit!" I marvelled, watching wide-eyed and wonderstruck as the two lusty ladies finger-fucked one another, woman-handled each other's knockers.

The girls went faster and faster. And I kept pace. They urgently pumped pussy and played with titty, recklessly and relentlessly driving one another to the boiling brink of orgasm, driving me right over the edge.

My senses overloaded with the sight and sound and

smell of those two breast-blessed babes lezzing like crazy. "Fuck almighty!" I bellowed, jerking thick ropes of sizzling semen out of my raging cock.

Mary and Lola cried out their own ecstasy, their lush, sweat-slick bodies shaking with orgasm. I saluted their blistering performance with one-handed fervour, spurt after spurt of sperm. Until at last my balls were empty and my cock sapped, the girls slumped together in each other's arms, boob to boob and nipple to nipple.

Lola was true to her word, unfortunately, and I never did get my paws or prick on either busty beauty again. But I've got a new route now. And there's this blonde, thirty-something office manager with a spectacular rack who's recently caught my attention …

24

# Phone On The Train
## by David Inverbrae

You are travelling on the train to meet me at my hotel. The train is busy and you text me to tell me how much you are looking forward to us exploring each other when you get to the end of your journey. I text you back and suggest we could start before you get there. I ask what you are wearing. You text back with a smiley face and tell me you are wearing my favourite grey suit, with lacy thong and front-fastening bra, holdups and four-inch heels, but that you are surrounded by people so won't be able to talk freely on the phone. I reply, telling you to put in your bluetooth earpiece and wait for my call.

I wait two minutes before calling … knowing that you will have been waiting with your finger on your phone button. Your phone is on vibrate, so when you feel my call coming in you immediately press the answer key but don't say a thing, waiting for me to speak, meaning that no one beside you on the train knows you are on the phone.

I tell you not to say anything and just listen as I tell you what I would do if we were alone in the carriage on the train. I would get you to stand up facing the carriage window, your hands wide apart and just above head-height pressed onto the glass … your feet wide apart to help you balance in those heels as the train bumps and jolts along the track at 70 miles an hour ... I would stand behind you ... kissing that spot on the back of your neck you like so much and then undo the buttons on your suit jacket. You would lean your head back as I nuzzle your neck ... my body pressing against yours from behind as my fingers undo the last button. You have only your lacy bra under the jacket and I tease your nipples though the lace, feeling them get harder as you push back against me to help you keep your balance ... letting you feel how hard I am as you press your hips back into my crotch.

You just sit there in the train surrounded by strangers as I describe how I would then unclip the front of your bra ... pulling the cups away from your breasts and then letting my hands take the place of your bra ... cupping your breasts in my hands and teasing your hardening nipples between my fingers ... then suddenly the train jolts and I push you against the glass, the tips of your stiff nipples pressing against the cold of the glass as my hot fingers squeeze your breasts, forcing them to make circular patterns on the window.

Then I tell you how I would lower myself down onto my knees behind you, your feet are already quite wide apart meaning that the tight skirt of your suit has already ridden up your thighs. Your body is swaying with the motion of the train making your nipples slide all over the glass of the window. I put my hands on the side of your skirt and start to push it higher, revealing first the smooth skin of your thighs at the top of your holdups and finally, as I push your skirt up over your hips, the back of your white lacy thong ... the string lost between your buttocks, and the lacy fabric moulded tight over your crotch making the groove of your pussy lips clearly outlined in the material. I would run my hands over your buttocks, kneading and massaging and separating them. You would push them back at me … still with your breasts hard against the glass. My finger would trace the line your pussy makes in the lace and you would let out a soft moan as I press harder, feeling your heat and dampness, pushing the material between your lips so your thong is like a string pressing against your clit. I pull the back of your thong away from your cheeks, using the elastic of the material to let it run back and forwards against your clit as the train moves, your lips opening a little now and starting to glisten in the lights of the carriage.

I tell you I would give a sharp tug and the thong snaps, leaving you naked from the waist down except for your stockings and heels. I would lean forwards and start to blow on your pussy from behind and then start to lick you, pulling your cheeks apart so I can get my face in further and lick and suck on your clit and lips, my tongue flicking your clit and then wriggling inside your pussy … exploring inside you. Then I tell you how I would sit on the floor with my back to the side of the carriage, your clit in front of my face … swollen and wet. I pull your hips towards me and start to suck on your clit. You would begin moving your hips, grinding your clit into my mouth, my fingers probing you from behind, one teasing your bum hole and two others sliding easily into your soaking pussy as the train starts to slow.

I glance out of the corner of my eye, thinking I might need to stop if we are approaching a station but it seems to be just slowing to a walking pace and I realise it is because there are workmen at the side of the road. I keep sucking your clit and fingering you, wondering how you will react when you see the workmen through the window and knowing they will be able to see you. But I tell you that you would respond by pushing harder onto my mouth and then whispering "please fuck me!!!!" I would get up and stand behind you. The men have started walking along the track beside our window. Your thighs are wet from my mouth and your juices and you balance yourself against the window with one hand ... squeezing your nipples with the other for the men to see. I slip my cock into you from behind and you groan. The men's eyes are on your hand, and you bring it down to your pussy, pulling your lips clear of your clit so you can expose it to them and let them see my cock sliding in and out of you from behind. You push back on me as I go in deeper and then pull me forwards by thrusting your hips against the window. You gasp as your clit hits the cold glass and you start to cum ... begging me to cum at the same time. You feel me jerk inside you, straightening my knees and forcing you off your feet as I drive deep into you, making your clit slide up the glass as we cum together ... our juices dribbling out of you and trickling down the window in front of the amazed gaze of the workmen just as the train begins to speed up again.

All the time I've been telling you this down your mobile, I've been listening to your breathing, noticing how it has changed, and knowing just by the sound of you that you are very aroused at the thought of what I had been describing. I tell you that I'm lying waiting for you in our hotel room and then ask if you are feeling sexy now. "Yes" you breathe down the phone. I ask if you are still surrounded by people and again you answer "Yes". Then I ask if you think they know how aroused you are, if you've been squirming in your seat and if your nipples are hard and showing? "Yes" again comes your reply, so I tell you to open your knees a little and slide forward on your seat so your skirt rides up. "OK" is your

28

one-word reply and your breathing gets harder. "Is there a guy opposite you and is he watching you?" I ask. "Yes" again. I tell you to watch his face and to open your knees a bit wider.

"Is he looking?"

"Yes."

"Slide forward a bit more."

"Yes."

Then you whisper, "He's dropped his phone and having to pick it up". I tell you to open wider now and let him see your lacy panties glued to your pussy. The guy opposite bends over to pick up the phone but takes his time, his eyes glued to your crotch and then it dawns on you that he's using the phone to photograph you.

Just then I can hear the squeal of the brakes as the train pulls into the next station. I know it's not the one you're getting off at yet and I hear commotion as people get up and leave. Then you tell me that the carriage has just emptied and the train has just pulled out again so you can talk properly. I ask you if it is dark enough outside that you can see your reflection in the window. You tell me you can, so I tell you to twist round in your seat and put your foot nearest the window up on the seat so you get a good view of what I am going to tell you to do. I tell you to stroke your finger along your thong just like I had told you I would and then bunch the fabric between your lips … then I tell you to pull the material back and forwards against your clit again … Then I hear you gasp … "OH GOD …. HE'S BACK!!"

I ask you what you mean and you tell me that the guy who had been photographing you with his phone had sneaked back into the carriage and has just sat down in the corner seat opposite you. I ask you if you are still sitting the same way and you tell me you are. I tell you to pull your thong away so he can see everything, then I tell you to use your first and third finger to open your lips and then tease your clit with the tip of your middle finger. You tell me he has his phone out ... I tell you to "Ask him if it does video". I hear you ask and then him replying that it does. I tell you to start to finger yourself, using one hand to hold your thong away and two fingers inside your pussy slowly moving in and out so he can get a good view and rub your clit with your thumb at the same time. I can tell from the little noises you are making in the back of your throat that you are doing exactly what I am telling you to do. Then I tell you to circle your bum hole with your pinkie and finally you groan as I tell you to slip your pinkie inside ... "I'm going to cum!!" you moan down the phone and I listen as you start to cum, your breathing changing to short gasps, then almost yelps as you make yourself cum in front of the stranger with the video phone.

Just as your breathing starts to settle ... you feel the train start to slow. You pull off your thong and hand it to the guy as you stand up and smooth your skirt down over your thighs. As you leave the carriage you are surprised to see me standing on the platform waiting for you. We kiss and I can feel the heat from your body. As the guy with the phone looks on, you put your fingers to my face and I can smell your pussy on your fingers, my tongue flicking out and slowly licking them. Just as well the hotel is only two minutes away.

# FantasyX
## by Penelope Friday

It was fantasy night. Dee could hardly breathe with anticipation as she waited for Kyle to come home. It was nearly a month since their last game, and this one had been spoken of a couple of weeks previously and never mentioned again. It felt more exciting that way, and Dee knew Kyle would remember the details she had whispered to him in the middle of that night, when she had spilled one of her deepest, most shocking, fantasies to him.

Kyle. Her heart thudded that little bit faster as she pictured her husband. He was so sensual, so powerfully sexual – and he saved it all for her. Other women noticed his good looks but they had no idea how hot he could be.

Dee grinned, remembering the overheard conversation earlier that day. She'd been at the photocopier when she heard voices outside the window; Julie and Carrie, having their usual sneaky fag.

"So, I saw Kyle again yesterday. I don't think he knows the difference between a woman and one of his blessed computers, from the notice he took of me." (Julie had slept with five of the male members of staff to Dee's knowledge, though it might be more, and took lack of interest as a personal affront.)

"He wouldn't, would he – he's married to Dee!" Both women squealed with laughter. "So sweet," Carrie continued maliciously; "they were school sweethearts, you know, before they both started working here. Probably virgins till the day they married.

"Probably virgins still," said Julie. "Or do you think he has a timer on his home computer? 'Beep beep,' time to have sex now. 'Beep, beep,' time to finish."

"D'you think it's two minutes of missionary position every Friday night? Highlight of the week?"

"Or lowlight," Julie rejoined.

Dee had listened to the conversation, greatly entertained. Probably, she should have been offended, but the two girls were so wide of the mark she had found it difficult to hold back her laughter. Did they know how bitter and jealous they sounded – without even knowing how much they had to be jealous about?!

He would be home soon. Dee checked her watch, then glanced in the mirror to ensure her hair and make-up looked right. For the nth time she smoothed a hand over her hair then sat down; stood up; sat down again. Hell, she was really nervous! She'd had this fantasy for so long, and even after they first began swapping stories and acting them out … well, she never imagined she'd be able to tell even him about this one. But she trusted him, and it was excitement as well as nerves that were making her shiver. Tonight – tonight, Kyle was going to take control. She would submit, obey his every word, willingly – wantonly – dominated by her man. She would be Kyle's play-thing, his toy and have no mind of her own; she would be bent to Kyle's will. Whatever Kyle asked. *Whatever*. She crossed her legs tightly, tingling with desire.

The key turned in the lock and Dee felt her heart rate

spike.

"Kyle?"

"Mm-hmm."

The sitting room door opened and Kyle walked in. Dee took a deep breath. Wow, he certainly knew how to dress the part. The tingling increased as she looked from the leather jacket to the sharp-cut jeans (lingering appreciatively at his crotch) and down to the polished boots. He looked at her in turn and lifted an eyebrow.

"Aren't you supposed to stand up when I'm in the room, little submissive? I expect good manners in you. You surely don't need to be punished for disobedience this soon? I'm disappointed in you."

Dee was getting to her feet before he had finished speaking.

"Sorry, Kyle."

He strode over to her and held her face firmly by the chin.

"That's *master* to you," he said coldly.

"Yes, master," she breathed.

His grip loosened and he smiled.

"Good girl. Now, I've bought you a present. Stay there."

She stood where he left her, absolutely still and barely daring to move a muscle. Who knew what Kyle might do to her if she moved without permission? The thought alone was erotic and she was almost tempted to move just to see; but Kyle returned before she had a chance and her eyes widened at what she thought she glimpsed in his half-concealed hand.

"Kneel," he ordered; and she was on her knees in front of him.

He brought his hand round into full view and she saw she had not been mistaken in that stolen glance  He held a leather collar.

"Undress for me, Dee." The note of command stayed in his voice, but she felt herself flushing at his unconcealed excitement. She tried to stand up, but his hand on her shoulder pinned her down. "No. Stay there. You will undress at my feet."

Her gaze meeting his, she began to unbutton her flimsy white blouse. She slid it off and reached her hands behind her, rushing to unhook her bra.

"Skirt next," Kyle instructed.

"Yes, master."

It was a struggle to remove the skirt from her kneeling position but Kyle showed no signs of relenting and allowing her to stand. His face was impassive but the bulge in his trousers, so near to her face, told a different story. Wriggling free at last, she gave him an inquiring look, not daring to speak.

"Yes, everything," he said softly.

Her bra was unclasped and discarded; panties followed. She was nude. She was naked and he was fully clothed: the ultimate signal of supremacy.

"Very good," he drawled. He bent over her and fastened the collar around her neck. "Listen to me, Dee, while you wear this collar you are under my command. You will submit to my every order, every … whim. Until it is removed, I call the shots Understand?"

"Yes, master," she said obediently.

The collar served two functions, she realised. First as a symbol of her status in the power play, but secondly as her safety net. All the time she wore the collar she must obey. But if she removed it, the game was over. It signified her own element of control, and highlighted more than anything else why she both loved and trusted Kyle.

"Thank you, master."

He took her hand and raised her to her feet.

"Look at yourself," he instructed.

She walked to the mirror, aware all the time of Kyle's eyes raking her body. The woman she saw staring back at her from the glass was a shock even to herself. Dee had never considered herself even average-looking, let alone beautiful. But a young, sultry reflection looked out at her. Huge, dark eyes; cheeks flushed a suggestive pink; a mouth begging to be plundered. Then, further down, full and heavy breasts tipped with hard coral-coloured nipples, which thrust themselves forward. There was the faintest line from her summer tan, showing how modestly she'd dressed out of doors that August; but there, an inch wide, contrasting darkly with her pale throat, sat the collar. Kyle's mark of possession. Dee's fantasies had never included such an item: now, looking at the sensual woman in the mirror, she could not imagine this fantasy without it. It was perfect.

"Do you like what you see, Dee?"

Kyle came up behind her and caught her reflection's eye. He ran a possessive hand down her arm. The touch of his fingertips was like an electric shock on her bare skin. She jolted, taking a deep, indrawn breath. He moved closer, pulling her against him so that her back rubbed against the smooth-rough surface of his jacket. She could smell the musty leather, and she leaned her head back against his shoulder with sensuous enjoyment. One of his legs pushed between hers, and his hands moved up to cup her breasts. He stroked the pads of his thumbs against her engorged nipples and she whimpered in pleasure.

"Yes, you like that," said Kyle appreciatively. "I like it too." He pulled her further onto his leg, so that she

35

could feel the pressing weight of his erection against her bottom. "Can you feel how much I like it?"

"Oh, yes!"

And Kyle's mood appeared to change in an instant at her words. He pushed her away and down to her knees again.

"Yes – what?" he demanded.

"Master."

She bowed her head in mute apology. He bent down and ran a finger over her collar before thrusting a booted foot in front of her.

"Lick."

She glanced up uncertainly. Did he really mean her to …? Once more his face was expressionless. She could stop this at any time, but she didn't – oh, she *really* didn't – want to. She grovelled at his feet, planting kisses on the polished surface of his boot. Above her, she could feel him moving slightly, and when she looked up she saw that he had undone his flies and allowed his erection to spring free.

"Yes, you know what to do next, Dee," he encouraged her.

She had always loved fellatio, from their earliest sexual encounters as teenagers when the fear of pregnancy had made intercourse as terrifying as it was enthralling. She loved the feel – the weight – the taste of him in her mouth, loved the twin feelings of vulnerability (increased tenfold by her present position and nakedness) and control. And Kyle did something he rarely tried, tangling his fingers through her hair to remind her that even now, her mouth around his cock, it was he who held the power. She encircled the head with her tongue before moving her lips wider to take him all in, into her mouth until he touched the back of her throat. Then she moved, urged thereto by the pressure of his hands on her head, by his softly muttered words of encouragement and praise.

"There, there; that's it, my submissive one, you know what you're doing. Yes, Dee, come on, you know how."

One of her hands was on the inside of his thigh, the other reaching up to grab his arse. She knew just what he liked and wanted to give him everything, but he held her back, fingers firm in her hair, though his ragged breathing betrayed the fact he was close to the edge.

"No, Dee. I want to take you. I want to come inside you while you're begging me to fuck you."

Dee found her hand reaching between her own legs at his words. Kyle didn't say things like this usually – not her Kyle – but she found herself hopelessly turned on by this new, masterful version of her husband. He slapped her hand away.

"No touching yourself unless I say, Dee."

"Yes, master."

A small smile crept across his lips.

"But now that you've put the idea in my head … yes, go on, little one. Show me what you do to yourself. Show me how you pleasure yourself when you're all alone. Put on a little show for me, hmm?"

She wanted to and she didn't want to, but not in equal amounts. The desire, the need to touch herself was making her almost dizzy. One hand reached down, the other fondling her breasts (first one then the other) almost unconsciously whilst her main attention concentrated on that nub between her legs. She was warm and wet, intensely aware of Kyle watching her. She started with a light touch, but as her need increased her fingers worked faster, firmer …

"Now stop," Kyle ordered.

Dee moaned, not wanting to halt now when she was

37

so close, but Kyle's fingers were touching her collar, reminding her of her duty of obedience, and reluctantly she took her hands from her body.

"Get on all fours."

She gave him a last look, to remember everything about this moment. Kyle, still fully clothed, standing over her, his eyes dark with lust and love. God, how she wanted him. She crouched on all fours, and felt him kneel behind her. He explored with his fingers for a second, then, as she begged for more, he pushed inside her. Digging his fingernails into her shoulders, he whispered,

"What do you want, Dee?"

She knew what he meant. She would have to ask – to plead – for his attentions.

"You," she murmured.

"Why, I'm here!" he teased, moving with tantalising gentleness inside her.

"More," Dee insisted.

Kyle kept his light motion up, laughing under his breath.

"Oh, I think you'll have to ask me more nicely than that," he said.

"Kyle – master – *please*," she begged; then, as he waited for more, she added "Please, fuck me. Please."

He ran his nails down her spine, and she arched her back at his touch.

"Since you ask so pleasingly, how could I refuse?"

And he was thrusting, thrusting into her; and she – she was rocking back and forth, increasing the tempo, increasing the pressure, caring for nothing but arriving at that point of ecstasy. And then it came, and she tumbled over it, crying a wordless litany of bliss before she felt him shudder inside her as he reached his own peak.

Afterwards, they lay together on the floor, arms round each other. Kyle reached up and removed her collar with gentle fingers.

"Darling," he said, "you were wonderful." He smiled. "I don't think we'll throw this away yet, either."

And she knew that her fantasy had worked its magic on him.

# Any Friend Of Hers
## by Jeremy Edwards

Dahlia was so excited at the prospect of having her three
closest friends converge on us for a dinner party that I
could hardly keep up with her. As always, I was a good
person to have on the team for menu planning, music
selection, and determining which napkins to use. But
there was an electricity in the air that wasn't quite
capturing me. Maybe it was because these were primarily
Dahlia's friends, and I really didn't know any of them
that well.

I'm not the type of husband who deliberately
segregates his pals and his interests from those of his
partner, nor is Dahlia that type of wife. Ideally, we prefer
to enjoy things together – be it activities, places, or
people. Yet for one reason or another, circumstances had
resulted in her forming close friendships with a few
women that I never saw much of. She had met Nicole
through a reading group, for example. (Personally,
though I love books, I can't stand reading groups. "Shut
up and let me read" is my attitude, and this is not a polite
position to articulate at a book-club meeting.) Camille
was a long-time colleague of Dahlia's, and Alexandra
was her physician. Sure, Dahlia and I had shared some
nice evenings out with each of these friends. But busy

schedules meant that Dahlia's interactions with them were most often in the context of quick mid-day lunches or "catch-up-on-everything-in-five-minutes-or-less" telephone calls. So I usually had to settle for second-hand updates, brought home by Dahlia with the leftovers from lunch.

When I returned from work on Friday, Dahlia was in our spare room, aka the "junk room". I was surprised to find her engaged in some restorative maintenance to her wig collection – a five- or six-piece assortment, dating back to her days as a principal player in a local repertory theatre company.

"Nostalgic?" I whispered, as I wrapped my arms around her middle and pressed against her from behind.

Dahlia laughed a laugh of sincere happiness, which seemed to light up all the manifold junk in the junk room. "No," she said briefly. "Don't miss the stress. Still enjoying the outcome." The "outcome" had been that just as the rep company was closing its doors, her relationship with a certain lucky guy became serious – and permanent. She had never regretted the turn of events that had suddenly left her evenings free.

With sentiment ruled out, I attributed the wig maintenance simply to Dahlia's good habit of taking proper care of things. They don't hire just anybody as a museum curator, and this was exactly what she had become after the theatre's final season. But the curatorial wig duties that I had interrupted were to be put on hold for about thirty minutes. Dahlia melted and wriggled sweetly in my arms, and we drifted casually but purposefully out of the junk room and into the bedroom.

"Do you ever sort of want to fuck my friends?"

It was a strange question to hear on a Saturday

41

morning. Consequently, it was a struggle for me to swallow rather than eject the mouthful of coffee that Dahlia's query had overtaken.

"Huh?" I laughed. "Last I knew, this was a monogamous relationship." I looked around from left to right, as though expecting extraneous women to emerge from the pantry or laundry chute.

Dahlia leaned across the breakfast table to give me a light kiss. "I know. That's why I'm saying 'sort of'." She smiled understandingly. "I don't mean would you seriously, solemnly desire to go to bed with my buddies, in 3-D and real time. I just mean ...does it ever cross your mind, in an idle way, as an appealing scenario?"

"Oh. Well ... sure. I suppose."

Her eyes lit up with interest. "Which ones? If you don't mind my asking."

Of course I didn't mind. We have no secrets from each other.

I shrugged. "All of them, now that you mention it. You have good taste."

She kissed me again, quickly, as she stood up. "Oops – I'd better get going." And, in an instant, she was out the door. But I could swear that she had favoured me with a split-second salacious wink, right before disappearing.

She was headed to the mall, where she had arranged to meet Camille, Alexandra, and Nicole. None of them were shopping fanatics; but they also weren't blind to the attraction of the occasional spiffy new ensemble. For ages now, they had all been too busy to try on clothes, and Dahlia had suggested they use the dinner party as an excuse to rectify this. "We're going to shop all together," she had explained to me, shortly before asking if I ever sort of wanted to fuck her friends – and in pretty much the same tone of voice. "The plan is for each of us to find one outfit. Then we're going to wear them at dinner tonight."

"Do I need a new outfit?" I had inquired. I wouldn't have objected to sporting a new outfit, in principle. However, the men's clothes that I happen to find aesthetically appealing all went out of fashion several decades ago, around the time I was born. I've often wished that my parents had stocked up on grown-up clothes for me while I was still an infant, instead of plying me with those extra twenty or thirty stuffed animals.

"They won't have anything you like, sweetheart." How well she knows me.

"I don't really have the time, anyway," I had acknowledged, while giving her bare knee a squeeze under the table. "Otherwise, I would have been happy to tag along, just to watch you try things on." I had yet to acquire the requisite groceries for the evening, a task I would of course have to tackle before I could even begin to transform said groceries into anything that could loosely be described as 'dinner'. Yes, as tonight's designated chef, my day was spoken for. There would only be five of us – Nicole and Alexandra were both single at the moment, and Camille's husband was out of town – so this would not be an immense undertaking. Still, I knew from experience that I'd probably do one or two stupid things in the kitchen, before finally transcending my inherent, pathetic clumsiness with my intrinsic culinary genius. And the repercussions of the stupid things usually added at least an hour to the prep time – not to mention complicating the clean-up.

These were four very efficient and discriminating women, and they had shopped effectively. Dahlia looked good enough to eat in her peach cocktail dress, her pageboy of light brown hair kissing her gorgeous neck. Each of our guests arrived in something equally striking, and carefully selected for its ability to harmonize with her individual loveliness. For Nicole, whose vivid red curls made many colours risky, it was a silk sleeveless top in a delectable shade of cream, worn with a short black skirt. A slit up the side of the skirt revealed a sassy thigh. Alexandra, who was only a quarter Japanese but whose ultra-straight, ultra-black hair had arrived intact as a legacy from her grandmother, looked fresh as a flower in a jade blouse and form-fitting plum slacks. Soft, round eyes and a button nose added an element of cuddliness to her statuesque beauty. And Camille's long blonde locks gave the perfect bohemian effect with the low-cut paisley gown she'd chosen. Above her handsome cleavage, freckles danced merrily across the vicinity of her collarbone, resonating with the multicoloured joy of the dress.

It was an engaging little soirée. As we dined, drank and relaxed, I had the opportunity to further appreciate why my wife was so fond of these lively, intelligent friends. I was tickled by Nicole's sardonic wit, seduced by Alexandra's air of shy mischief, and moved by Camille's passionate zest for art and beauty. Each woman had her own way of filling the room with grace and delight. And what fitting companions they all were for my Dahlia, whose personal combination of warmth and playfulness twinkled exquisitely throughout the party.

Our guests were absolutely charming. And yet I'm not sure I would have spent quite so much time observing how beautiful they all were, if it hadn't been for the question Dahlia had asked me that morning. As it was, my mind kept digressing into creative visions of the three

44

women, in various erotic poses. Within the realm of these mini-fantasies, I saw myself mingling with each of them. I could vividly imagine the textures of all their garments as I drew aside blouses, slacks and skirts to squeeze or caress the delicious, bare expanses that I knew lay within. My evening was undeniably enhanced by this luscious dimension to my thoughts – a gift from Dahlia.

"That was so much fun," I said to her after the company had departed and the place had been tidied up. "What a good idea of yours."

"I'm full of good ideas," she answered significantly. "And the fun has only begun."

I had hoped that she might be horny for some after-party frolicking, and her manner indicated that my hopes were coming to life. But I had no hint of the ingenious treat she had planned for us, until we entered the bedroom.

She had been busy in here while I'd been cleaning up in the kitchen. As a result of her efforts, the room had been prepared for what could best be described as a show. I swallowed hard as I took it all in.

On a couple of chairs by the window were draped three outfits. They were identical to the outfits that had been seen tonight on Nicole, Alexandra, and Camille.

"After lunch at the mall today, I said goodbye to them and then retraced our steps," Dahlia whispered in my ear. In other words, she had gone back and made a duplicate purchase of each of their outfits, so that she could play dress-up with me.

Then I saw that across the room on the bureau were three of Dahlia's wigs, poised perfectly atop their stands. One was a curly red wig that recalled Nicole; one wig was straight and black like Alexandra's hair; and one was a generous wig of blonde that approximated Camille's distinctive mane. So this was why Dahlia had been attending to her wigs yesterday.

My eyes widened as I comprehended all that she was going to do. I embraced her, brushing her lips with a soft kiss of gratitude. I was tingling.

"Me first," she said.

And so I eased her onto the bed and busied myself with the delicious peach hem of her dress, wiggling it up high onto her hips. Dahlia had already removed her panties, and her sweet aroma complemented the peachy theme. She tasted like summer as I licked assiduously at her moist, tender pussy. It wasn't long before she cooed in girlish ecstasy and clamped her soft thighs around my cheeks.

I was so aroused at this point that I stood up, hastening to abandon my trousers and briefs. Meanwhile, Dahlia hopped off the bed and stripped. Her years in the theatre had taught her how to make quick changes, and in thirty seconds she had donned the "Nicole" outfit, complete with wig.

It was uncanny. In addition to her instincts and training, part of what had made Dahlia a capable actress was the flexibility of her features. As soon as she was dressed as Nicole, she set her face into an expression that truly evoked her friend's attitude-tinged radiance. It really almost felt as if I were about to get it on with Nicole, rather than Dahlia. But the deeply exciting thing was the prospect of bedding my own Dahlia while she *played* at being Nicole.

"Brava!" was all I could say.

Dahlia resisted the urge to speak. She is, of course, an excellent mimic and can imitate the voice of just about any woman she knows – and many of the men. Yet her judgment now told her that adopting an artificial voice could risk turning this moment from bedroom fantasy into bedroom comedy. So she settled for flashing me a wry, Nicole-esque smile. Then she wordlessly oozed her slit-skirted, silken-topped body into my arms.

At times this evening, as Nicole made us titter with her smart little quips, I had felt an idle urge to reach my hand up the slit in her skirt and fondle her shapely ass. Now, with this underwear-free pseudo-Nicole in my arms, I went to town. Her breasts pressed against me through the silk top, each nipple a hardened point of intimate contact, while I gave raunchy squeezes to the contours of her derrière. Eventually, I sent my hand underneath the cheeks to cup her honeypot. Juice dribbled onto my fingers as we navigated back onto the bed. "Nicole" clutched at my cock as we fell onto the mattress.

Courtesy of a classic 180-degree spin and some vigorous skirt-peeling, I soon found myself holding "Nicole's" bare legs above me, while she positioned her head in my lap. I took one thrilling look at her dazzling red curls as she went down on me. Then I grabbed her ass, lowered her crotch toward my mouth, and sank my face once again into the sweet spot.

Her cheeks vibrated in my hands as my tongue titillated her. Each of her pussy's wet shudders was seconded in my own vitals, as my prick danced to the soft rhythm of her lips and luxuriated in the velvety textures inside her mouth. As an image of the real Nicole crossing her legs on our couch a few hours ago flashed across my mind, I hugged the pillow of Dahlia's bottom and my sap exploded. While she drank me in, her sex juice washed like rain onto my face.

As soon as Dahlia had enough energy to bounce back off the bed, she shed the Nicole costume and dressed up like Alexandra. There she stood before me, a vision of jade and plum with jet-black hair, her face an expert imitation of Alexandra's enticing reticence. Then she turned to the dresser, bent her perfect plum ass my way, and took something out of the top drawer.

It was Dahlia's special tickle-feather, and no words were necessary for me to understand what she wanted. This was a favourite interlude of ours, when my cock needed a break. As the director of tonight's little performance, Dahlia had decided that what the shy, lovely character known as "Alexandra" craved was an erotic pampering with gentle tickles and miniature kisses. I had learned how to delight Dahlia in this fashion, and I relished the opportunity to pleasure "Alexandra" in the same manner, until her nipples would strain the soft fabric of her jade blouse and the crotch of her elegant plum slacks would grow slick with nectar. I thought of the actual Alexandra sitting quietly by our stereo, her face blissful as she basked in musical warmth, and how I had fantasized about kissing her cute nose. I imagined how she might have melted into precious bubbles of laughter if I had tickled her breasts through her thin shirt.

Dahlia's version of Alexandra sat silently on the edge of the bed. She unbuttoned the bottom few buttons of her blouse and lowered the zipper of her slacks a few inches, barely leaving her bush hidden. With her eyes, she directed my attention to her bare feet. Then she handed me the feather and pressed her eyelids closed. She let her arms go limp at her sides.

Experience had taught me exactly what was desired. I brushed her toes with the feather ever so slightly, and I watched her body respond with a sensuous shudder. I leaned in to kiss her exposed belly. Then I let the feather kiss the little triangle of flesh that peeked out from the

48

open zipper. "Alexandra" giggled erotically.

I kissed her fingers. I crouched down and tickled her toes again. I dusted her tummy lightly with the feather. As her ticklish wriggles evolved into gyrations of more intense arousal, I reached under her to feel the wetness that was developing. I stroked her there with my free hand. Before I could give her more than two or three more tickles, her giggles crescendoed into a shriek and I could feel her pussy throbbing warmly against me, coming hard. "Alexandra's" plum slacks were now a fragrant monument to Dahlia's momentous wetness.

She could hardly wait to be fucked. She flung the pussy-drenched pants aside, tore off the blouse, and slipped on the paisley gown, her erect breasts bouncing with anticipation as the dress slid onto her. Without even bothering to verify that she'd put the blonde wig on straight, Dahlia leapt at me. Her fiery eyes were at once a tribute to Camille's aura of artistic passion and to her own sizzling libido. And her ravenous lust was contagious. Over on my portion of the erogenous map, "Camille's" frenzy of sexual hunger finished the work that the tickle-play with "Alexandra" had begun. My cock was primed for fucking my wife into a woman's most heavenly state of real-life satisfaction, while my mind indulged in the latest round of make-believe.

Could the real Camille possibly be this wild in bed? I recalled her rapturous discussion of the Post-Impressionist paintings she'd seen on a visit to the Met. "There were so many important canvases I was wetting my pants," she had proclaimed at one point. She had looked so intense, so aglow in an almost-sexual way, that I'd actually wondered if her panties might be moist from the excitement of reliving her museum experience. I thought of that rapture and that moistness as I plunged

49

myself into Dahlia's squirming, panting impression of Camille. All was a blur of paisley and blonde as the heat of her cunt cooked me to perfection and I felt my consciousness dissolve into an echo of her throaty, orgasmic roars.

I woke up next to the Dahlia I was used to. She was asleep, her recently-protean face so distinctly her own as it lay in repose. In the best curatorial manner, she had put all the outfits away, including her peach dress. She was nude. She was beautiful. And she was all I wanted.

# Pigs
## by Lynn Lake

We were making out like a couple of police cadets, behind the billboard speedtrap on Highway 16, Rural Municipality of Foam Lake – finally. I'd been after the hunky rook ever since we'd been paired up together. But it'd taken me three long, hot and humid weeks to get the big stud where I wanted him – in my arms, tongues entwining.

Then the call came through, the cruiser's on-board computer beeping low-priority.

Constable Donovan Steele extracted his tongue from my mouth and said, "We'd better roll, Tanner," a spicy hint of the Islands in his deep voice.

"Call me Vicky," I breathed, massaging the muscleman's taut buttocks through his RCMP-issue blues. I painted his thick lips with my tongue, grinding my pelvis into his monster erection. "We'll follow up the call once we're done here. No big rush."

He gripped my shoulders and shoved me back against a billboard pillar, held me there, all business now, his green eyes sparkling and his ebony skin shining, fine-featured face set. I'd trained the guy too damn well.

"Duty calls," he growled, turning and striding away.

I watched his butt mounds tumble from side-to-side,

51

my pussy pulsing with need. The cruiser roared to life, and I ran a damp hand over my sweaty face and sighed, jogged toward the car. Donovan punched the accelerator, spraying gravel, as soon as my butt cleared the doorframe.

We fishtailed out from behind the 'Repent And Ye Shall Be Saved' sign and barrelled down the sun-blasted highway; two hungry cops cruising for trouble, smack-dab in the middle of the hog-country Bible Belt of rural Saskatchewan.

I scanned the text on the computer screen. Henry Hildebrande had filed a robbery complaint – two hundred of his pigs allegedly stolen. More hog-rustling. Three thousand porkers had gone missing in the past hotter-than-hell month, and the local farmers were raising a stink.

We skidded to a stop in front of the two-storey chartreuse farmhouse that fronted the Hildebrande Hogs operation. Henry Hildebrande materialized from the dust cloud, led us back to the corrugated-steel collection of barns that housed his piggery.

The ex-hippy turned swine plantation owner was decked out in a tie-dye T-shirt and a pair of plaid overalls, and a pork pie hat. "Two hundred of my fattest hogs – stolen!" he groused. He shoved back the pork pie, grey eyes a glassy concoction of many controlled substances.

The whole operation smelled to high heaven in the cloudless, hundred degree heat. Donovan whipped out a pad and a pencil and a line of questioning, while I kept downwind, kept my eyes on the young women crowding the screen door of the farmhouse, watching us.

"When did you first notice the hogs had gone

missing?" Constable Steele asked.

Hildebrande squinted up at my partner, fingering his grey knotted beard. "Seven this morning. When I sent one of the girls out to feed 'em."

Donovan nodded, jotted. I supervised, his superior by only six months (one graduating class). "Hear or see anything unusual?"

"Nope."

"Anyone else?"

"Nope."

"Any way to track the pigs – microchips, biometrics?"

"You mean like cars got VIN's – PIN's?" He laughed, pulled off the pork pie and mopped his face with a Grateful Dead doo-rag. "You gotta be kiddin' me. Some had ear tags, some didn't. I got five thousand head of hog here."

"Notice any tyre tracks or footprints, debris or equipment left behind by whoever perpetrated the crime?"

"Nope."

Donovan snapped the pad shut and pocketed the pencil, nodded. "We'll get your hogs back, Mr. Hildebrande, don't you worry. Mind if we take a look around?"

Hildebrande shook his head. "Pigs tracking pigs," he guffawed, then quickly added, "Stay outta the house and that green ... er, organic barn back there." He made tracks for the farmhouse, shooing the women back inside and latching the door.

Donovan and I poked around the place, but we found nothing more than hoofprints and tyre tracks from Hildebrande's pig hauler, the cut across the tread on one of the rear tires making it instantly recognizable.

"It's a tough one, Tanner," the twenty-two-year-old

53

rook commented, rubbing his dimpled chin and scanning the fallow fields that surrounded the hog plant.

"It stinks, all right. Let's get out of here," I said.

We made the rounds of the slaughterhouses, but there was nothing new there – no unusual shipments, unaccounted for spikes in volume, lost and/or forlorn-looking pigs. We got a cup of coffee and a basket of fresh eggs from the Boss at the Hutterite Colony operation, but that's all we got for our efforts. The temperature was rising, the scent of swine heavy in the air, but the trail of missing trotters was stone-cold.

We parked alongside the highway on the outskirts of Tuffnell, mauling things over while we waited for the report from HQ on all known local-area thieves and their last known activities and whereabouts. With no other leads, it was the usual suspects routine. Maybe we'd get lucky, shake a pig out of a poke.

"We could stake out some farms?" Donovan suggested.

"Too many farms, too few cops," I countered.

"A sting operation? Buy some hogs on the black market maybe?"

"There is no black market, only pink. The bearer of the pigskin entitled to the proceeds."

Donovan slammed his fist into his thigh. I reached over and rubbed the spot, kneading the heavy muscle of his quadriceps. Just one cop backing up another.

Then the computer screen flashed our list of suspects, and it was a long one. I lifted my hand and Donovan fired up the cruiser. We rolled down the shimmering asphalt towards our first address.

Until I spotted Two-four Tessio on a dusty secondary road, strolling along, shepherding a pig in front of him.

We pulled off the pavement and onto the gravel, in behind Tessio and his four-legged pal, piled out of the cruiser and into the blazing sun.

Two-four was a local-yokel career criminal, his nickname a testimony to his penchant for twenty-four-bottle cases of beer, which he invariably bought and drank in one sitting. He played both sides of the legal fence, busted and stooled an almost equal number of times. Brown-on-brown, he was built like the stubby precursor to today's more elongated barley sandwich container.

"Where're you and your boyfriend headed?" I asked the pig. The twin rows of nipples pegged her as a breeder sow.

Two-four eyed us nervously, laughed the same. It didn't take much to get this guy spilling his guts, literally and figuratively. "I just this minute found her, officer – walkin' 'long the road all by herself, eh. I just stopped to make sure she didn't get run over or nuthin', you know."

Two-four's rusted-out pickup was parked a hundred yards up the road, bed loaded with beer cases, tailgate hanging down like a tongue – thirsty for more cargo.

"Oh, yeah? Rumour is you've been hitting the casino at Longquill pretty hard lately," Donovan said, quoting from HQ's report. "Where'd you get the money, man?"

"Huh? What?" Two-four's greasy face dripped more than heat-related sweat.

Donovan stepped closer, looming big and mean and velvety-black and blue. My heart fluttered; Two-four's stopped.

"OK! OK!" he squealed, throwing his paws in the air. "I'm goin' halfers on a grow-op at SW37-25-28W. I –"

"Hold it!" I barked.

The sow was on the move, tip-toeing rapidly down the

road, perhaps disgusted with her companion, perhaps showing us the way to more missing piggies.

"In pursuit – south on Limit Road," Donovan breathed into his shoulder-mounted two-way.

We trailed after the pig, past Two-four's rust-bucket and down the yellow dust road. And two sweat-soaked kilometres later, the bristly pink quadruped led us not to a secret sty full of stolen hogs, but rather to an abandoned garbage dump that hadn't been fully bulldozed over. She buried her nose in the waller and went to town. I consoled my partner with a pat on the back, and the bum.

He turned to me, equal parts frustration and lust in his glittering, green eyes – a combustible mixture, to be sure. Then the he-cop grabbed me in his arms and savagely kissed me.

I knocked his hat off, kissed him back, rubbing his close-shaven head, swarming my tongue into his mouth. He grabbed my butt cheeks and squeezed, lifting me clear off the ground, our tongues fighting an erotic duel out there all in the open under the glaring sun.

We greedily kissed, French and otherwise, rubbing hard up against one another. Then Donovan tore apart the Velcro straps that bound my body armour and flung the protective gear aside, ripped open my tunic, exposing my chest. I popped my bra open, baring my breasts, and he bent his stubbled head down and licked at one of my florid nipples, sucked on it.

"Yes!" I moaned, the pig looking up from her snouting and sniffing the air.

Donovan kneaded my ass with one hand, squeezed a tit with the other, feeding on my nipples. He flogged first one over-engorged toggle with his coral-pink tongue and then the other. I held onto the guy's cinderblock shoulders and took it, loved it, revelling in the warm,

56

wicked feel of his wet tongue and mouth, his heavy hands. But when he went for my belt, I had to back him off.

"I know a place!" I gasped. "More private. Just a bit farther down the road."

He nodded, eyed the rooting pig. "Might as well, case is stalled anyway."

I reclothed, then drove hard and fast the kilometre up the road to Ben Kaski's old farm. Ben'd been a mixed grain farmer who'd given up the land when prices went bust, gone into the booming, semi-illegal Internet pharmacy biz, moving offshore to Antigua.

I led Donovan down the garden path and in behind the dilapidated barn. Then I shoved him onto his knees in the prairie tall grass, my body shaking with anticipation, the culmination of my cultivation of the raw and ready recruit.

He performed like a pro, unnotching and unzipping me with his long, deft fingers, pulling my pants and panties down. He gazed at my springy wetness for a moment, inhaling the tangy, needful scent. Then he moved his head closer, kissed my most intimate lips.

"Yes!" I groaned, slamming back against the weathered boards of the barn, my legs gone to rubber.

Donovan dug his fingers into my slit and pulled me apart, licked at my pink. His head bobbing up and down and his jade eyes fixed on me, he lapped and lapped at my pussy with his roughened tongue. I went body electric, my head spinning like a gumball siren.

He popped my clit up between his fingers and blew on it. But the big heat wasn't putting out any fires; he was flaming them.

"Suck it!" I hissed.

He twirled his tongue all around my puffed-up button,

57

setting me to shaking, before finally grinning and engulfing my nub with his lips. I clawed at the wood, blinking sweat from my eyes and staring wildly down at the Nubian god mouthing my treat.

He sucked and sucked on my clit, slapped it around with his tongue. He reached up for my boobs, and I tore off my body armour and tunic and bra and threw them aside. He grabbed onto my hanging tits. I grabbed onto his hands on my tits, the contrast of gleaming ebony on slickened ivory stunning, the kneading and squeezing and nipple-rolling exquisite.

My body temperature rocketed to the point at which pussy burns, my manhandled boobs tingling, my lip-locked clit coursing with impending ecstasy. I was forced to shove the guy back. He tumbled onto his ass in the grass. "Strip!" I growled.

He climbed to his feet and slowly disrobed, my hungry eyes following his every sensuous move. Until at last he stood in front of my heaving, dripping form in just his polished black boots and burnished black skin, his liquorice stick rising up in the breeze.

I pulled my baton out of my discarded belt, its night-shaded length surpassing Constable Steele by only a shade. I lifted the man's blue-black cap with the tip of the stick. He groaned, arms at his sides and back arched, cock straight out and jumping, as I bumped polished graphite back and forth on the veiny underside of his shaft, pressed club into his tightened balls.

"You're going to fuck me!" I told the rook, stroking cock with my nightstick.

He blinked his eyes and wet his lips and nodded.

I dropped the baton and sagged to the ground, onto my knees. I grabbed him, swirled my hand up and down the length of his pipe. He groaned, body jerking, cock surging in my hot little hand. I nipped at his hood, and he uttered an oath that had nothing at all to do with his duty to serve and protect.

"Suck me, Tanner!" he hissed.

"Vicky," I reminded him, before taking his swollen hood in my mouth and sucking.

He clutched at my hair, yanking my head forward, stuffing cock into my mouth. I clawed his ribbed stomach with one hand and tugged on his ball sack with the other, lips sliding back and forth on his shaft. He pumped his hips, fucking my mouth in rhythm to my sucking, a fast learner in every way.

But the man-cop had a hair-trigger, and only a minute or so in he was already ready to empty his rod in my throat. He popped out of my mouth before he exploded, though, rumbled, "You wanted to be fucked?"

I nodded up at him. Then I went down on all-fours, sticking my butt in the air like a female K9 in heat. And when he and his dangling cock were in the danger position behind me, I turned up the kink by saying, "Cuff me, motherfucker!"

He didn't ask questions, just pulled my arms behind my back and shackled me, eased me face-down into the grass. Then he whacked my trembling ass with his rubber hose of a cock, and I moaned something ludicrous like 'police brutality'. He really laid on the lumber then, smacking my fleshy mounds one at a time with his noirstick. I pushed up higher into the air, begging the hardcase to beat me on the inside.

"Here it comes, Vicky," he rasped, sticking fingers into my pussy and pumping, priming.

I shivered, hollered, "Fuck me!"

His fingers pulled out and a bulbous head pushed in, parting my lips, spearing inside me. I chewed grass, his

59

awesome shaft plunging into my pussy until balls kissed butt cheeks.

We both groaned with satisfaction. Then Donovan started moving his powerful hips, a hand on my waist and a hand on the cuffs, rocking me forward and yanking me back, pistoning full-length in my puss.

"Faster! Harder!" I cried, spitting dirt.

He churned my slot over and over, cocking me with reckless, relentless abandon, his body smacking hard and wet against my shuddering bum. He drove me into the ground, my head into orbit, until finally I yelled, "Uncuff me!" desperate to come when he came.

He fumbled the cuffs off my wrists and then went right back to pumping me, stretching my pink with his club. I grabbed at my clit and rubbed frantically, the both of us careening towards all-out release.

"I'm gonna come!" he bellowed, brutally pounding my cunt.

"Do it!" I bleated, polishing my button in a frenzy.

My body locked and then spasmed, my pussy exploding with fiery orgasm, shimmering ecstasy all through me. Donovan slammed into me, grunting his own joy, pulsing warm, wonderful semen into my being. We jerked around in the throes of our mutual orgasms. And then, amidst all the grunting and groaning and gushing: oinking.

Donovan collapsed over top of me, covering my wet, sizzling body with his. Still tremoring with orgasmic aftershocks, plugged together by pussy-embedded prick, we turned our weary heads and gazed at the pig. It was the same one we'd tracked on the road, judging from her dusty snout and body. She snuffed the sex-funked air and then turned curly tail and trotted off.

We staggered to our feet and dragged on our uniforms,

reconstituting ourselves as a Force and following after the rogue porker. She twinkle-toed into a clump of trees. And within those swaying birches and elms we found the drained pond that had once been the Kaski swimming hole. It was covered by a huge, patchwork tarp now. Beneath the tarp, rooting around on the dirt bottom of the shallow dugout: a herd of five hundred pigs or more. They looked up at us, squealing and squinting.

We held our noses and laid the edge of the tarp back down. My partner pointed at the tire tracks that led to the edge of the makeshift holding pen. "I recognize the cut in those treads," the big man in-uniform said, hands on his hips, justice on his lips.

We booked Henry Hildebrande on a hog-rustling beef that night, the Lab having no trouble matching up the pig trailer prints on his property with the ones at the clandestine pig-pond. The hippy-dippy hog farmer cracked shortly thereafter, shedding tears and squealing woe.

He needed money for his wives, he said – three ex's and five current. And the RM wouldn't give him the variance he needed to expand his piggery. So he'd gone hunting for cash on the hoof, wrangling hogs that weren't his and filing a false rustling report to cover his cloven tracks.

We all ended up with a headache, Hildebrande with a suspended sentence, Canadian justice being laxer than a girl's pussy after a good Donovan-reaming. And the polygamy charges weren't even considered, the Law being murkier on that touchy subject than an effluent lagoon.

Constable Steele and I received commendations from the Commissioner, however; certificates of appreciation from the RM Council. And I gave Donovan a sparkling fitness report, back behind the old, abandoned barn where all our probing investigative work had climaxed in success.

# Marie, Marie
## by Toni Sands

"You're joking!"

"Thank you, Tash. Glad you approve."

"But Marie – a geriatric guided tour when the world's your lobster? Imagine the Bahamas … Cuba … Copacabana." The last five syllables were a purr and I knew she was visualising hunks in trunks.

I played my ace. "My grand-dad fell in love with Canada when he worked there years ago. Now he's left me some money so I can see the country for myself."

The luxury road cruiser aka coach had delivered us to our Quebec hotel late the night before. The tour next morning blended power struggles and passion with today's cool city buzz. The vibrant murals and breathtaking buildings were a delight but my feet needed scratching. I told Judy I fancied a walk around the artists' quarter. She, and husband, Mike, had befriended me.

"If we don't see you before, we'll save you a seat on the boat," she said.

The 2.30 river cruise was part of the package and there was time for a wander before finding some lunch. I lingered over paintings and photographs crammed on to stall after stall; torn between a watercolour of maples in fall and a charcoal sketch of an ancient archway. Until a yellow awning glimpsed in a narrow street drew me towards a restaurant in a quieter area where the menu displayed outside was pure food porn.

Then he appeared. Beneath his pristine white apron he wore a black T-shirt and close-fitting dark trousers: the latter visible as I followed his delectable rear view through the restaurant where doors led to a sheltered patio. He seated me under a giant fern tree and while I sipped wine my eyes followed him as he weaved between tables. Now and then he darted a glance at me; a faint smile playing on his shapely lips. Once or twice he brushed past me; the brief contact tantalising my nerve-endings. My love life at that point was a desert but my imagination was concocting sizzling desserts as I ate a salad tossed in heaven and served with warm ciabatta.

When Mr Fabulous brought coffee, he paused. "Excuse me, M'selle. Are you on holiday?

"Touring. We're here for two more nights."

He placed a business card beside my cup. "Perhaps you will visit my restaurant again."

One smouldering glance and he whisked away to greet more diners. Fine. So all he was after was repeat business. Ah well, a girl can dream. I finished my coffee and approached the pay desk. Mr Fabulous was there before me. And his gaze told me I had to return.

I caught up with Judy and Mike as they were climbing the gangplank of the River Princess. We found three deck chairs by the rail and Mike went in search of cold beers. I hoped Tash, back home in Brighton, wasn't shedding tears for me. The scenery slid by in the sunshine as the guide, in seventeenth century dress, commentated in French and English. We sailed past a waterfall called the Bridal Veil and I was thinking how the guide's ruffled

64

shirt so resembled the cascade when his treacle tones together with the French lager began their seduction. Behind my shades, my eyelids were closing. And nothing could prevent me fantasising about the sexy restaurateur with the scrumptious menu.

What if I'd lingered at the bistro and missed the river trip? What if all the other diners left, leaving the proprietor and me alone? What if he had brought wine and two glasses then put up the 'Closed' sign? At this thought, my nipples pushed against my silky top as if inviting his fingers to find them. Meanwhile, in dreamland, my own hand was wandering too. Those tight trousers of his were peeling off to reveal …

"Ladies and Gentlemen, we will be docking in a few minutes. We trust you have enjoyed your cruise along the mighty St Lawrence." The PA system crackled. Passengers collected belongings.

Back on the coach, Judy tapped my shoulder. "Fab day but I'm cream-crackered. D'you fancy coming out for a meal with Mike and me tonight? Escape from the hotel? We'd enjoy your company."

"Great. Love to, thanks. Actually, I know a brilliant restaurant."

Seated inside Chez Guy that evening, I tried to play down my anticipation.

"That slinky red dress is great with your dark hair," Judy said.

There was no sign of Guy but Mike was having difficulty averting his gaze from my cleavage.

While he was studying the wine list, Judy nudged me. "Maybe I'll be on a promise tonight?"

The pair of us giggled as we tried to concentrate on

the menu. I was lucky with my fellow travellers on this 'geriatric coach trip'. But would my luck hold or was it Guy's night off?

Then he was standing beside me, notepad in hand. A whiff of leather and musk tugged at my nostrils. I had to dig my nails into my palm to prevent myself from touching his thigh beneath those tailored trousers. Mike was consulting Judy about the wine and my tummy lurched as Guy bent to whisper in French. I understood only the word *belle*. Oh, why had I not paid more attention at school?

The meal progressed. I became more and more turned on. While the other two discussed next day's whale-watching trip, I found that by nodding and saying a word here and there, I could continue the daydream featuring me, Guy and the strawberries.

*He was dipping each berry in wine before slipping it between my lips. He was wearing nothing but a leather thong. I wore panties; a silken wisp that he could easily tease down my thighs. I watched him select another strawberry and soak it in wine. He opened his mouth. He bent his head and I felt the fruit, cool and slightly rough, graze my clitoris. I sighed as Guy gently nibbled and sucked until the berry was gone ...*

"Are you too hot, pet? Could you open the window, Mike? Marie's looking quite flushed here." Judy turned to me. "You must cover up tomorrow. I think you've caught the sun."

My fantasy would have to wait until I was alone in my room. Our main courses arrived. Wine flowed. I was having fun. Maybe my sex life was better played out in my mind rather than for real. But, oh, how I hoped that Guy might have his own views on that matter.

Mike settled the bill with a waiter so I didn't see Guy

until we were on our way out. He kissed Judy's hand when she complimented him on the food. Then, turning to me, he raised my hand to his lips and I found my fingers closing on whatever he'd pressed into my palm. While we were walking back to our hotel, Mike's attention was drawn to a sex shop window. Much as I'd have enjoyed checking out the vibrators, I moved up the street to join Judy who was ogling an imaginative display of male underwear.

When the lift reached my floor I could hardly unlock my room fast enough. As I read the note Guy had pushed into my hot little hand, I was practically creaming.

*Dinner tomorrow night? Please come to Chez Guy at 7.00 pm.*

The group meal was tomorrow evening: our last night in Quebec. I'd have to invent a plausible excuse not to attend. Because this was one unmissable invitation. I could feel that husky voice echoing around my body.

I unzipped my dress, my reflection smiling at me from the mirror. I was bra-less so I hooked my fingers in my briefs, wriggled out of them and reached for some scented gel. I let it spurt on to the palm that Guy had kissed. Moistening my nipples released such a craving that I lay on the bed, legs apart. My mind was racing as my fingers coaxed and spun me towards orgasm. I balled my fist against my slit and shuddered with pure delight. Pussy time alone was fun. The prospect of a liaison with Gorgeous Guy was breath-taking.

Next morning at the breakfast buffet, Judy smiled knowingly when I explained I'd dropped out of the group meal.

"I hope this means you've got a date."

"Um ...well ...sort of ..."

67

"Good girl," she said. "A looker like you was bound to pull in this fabulous city. Now I know it's safe to walk alone here at night, but why not programme my number into your mobile? Then you can ring us if you need to. But only if you need to." She winked and spooned more mango into my dish. "Must keep your strength up."

All day, even while exclaiming over the porpoises and minke whales, my thoughts were fast forwarding. And back at the hotel, as I showered and dressed for the evening, my excitement grew as I sprayed perfume on pulse spots. My senses seemed heightened by every whisper of flimsy fabric as I arranged my breasts in a white push-up bra and stepped into skimpy white knickers. I chose an emerald green, high-neck sleeveless top over white trousers. My shag-me scent – Tash's description, not mine – lingered around me as I pushed my bare feet into strappy sandals. I arrived in the foyer just as the coach was pulling away, transporting the group to a speciality restaurant. I wondered what special item Guy would offer, now that I'd opted for his alternative menu.

People were strolling or relaxing in cafés as I passed through the archway into the old city with its continental atmosphere. By contrast, Chez Guy looked forlorn, its pavement tables and chairs removed. I wondered if the bistro always closed on a Sunday night. Surely Guy would not have missed a night's trading on my account? My heart beat faster as I tried the ornate latch without success. But there was a soft glow from the shadowy interior as I peeped through a window. The heavy door swung open to reveal Guy. He took my hand and drew me inside.

"I am so glad you came," he said. As the door closed behind me I decided that it was obscene for a man to

68

have such sensuous lips and sooty eyelashes, but who was I to complain? A table for two was laid near the fireplace. An urn filled with white flowers gleamed against the dark stone. Guy must have been pretty certain I'd turn up. But any red-blooded male would have known it was not just the sumptuous food making me drool the previous evening. I wondered who was responsible for the many chic touches in the restaurant. Maybe Guy's talents extended in all sorts of directions? A suit of armour stood to one side of the fireplace and candles in wall sconces cast splashes of light. I was in an ancient building, history oozing from its pores and … Guy was holding out a glass containing a pale gold liquid.

"Un aperitif?" Even my schoolgirl French could cope with that. But the sparkle in his eyes spoke of more things than food to follow. A shiver trawled down my spine as I sipped the delicious drink, unsure of the flavour.

"Melon cordial with sparkling wine," he said. "But now it is my turn to ask you a question, Marie?"

I couldn't remember telling him my name. He must have heard Judy and Mike using it. "Go on."

He drank from his glass, still holding my gaze. "I wondered what your expectations were, when you decided to come here tonight – apart from supper, of course."

Was this some sort of test? I obviously wasn't here merely to hold hands with him … not with the luxury road-cruiser scheduled to leave Quebec next morning at 8 a.m.. And wasn't I a woman of the world?

"We both know this can only be a one-night stand, Guy. It will be what we make of it."

He reached out his free hand and rubbed his thumb gently over the bare flesh above my waistband. I shivered

– caught cradling my glass and with an electric thrill streaking straight to my core.

He laughed softly and put down his glass. "Enjoy your drink, *chérie*." He cupped my face between his hands and brought his mouth within kissing distance so that I felt the warmth of his breath. I swayed a little in my frivolous sandals and he encircled my waist with his hands, steadying me. As if that were possible …

"It is almost time to begin," he whispered.

But he had promised me dinner and while I drained my glass, he disappeared briefly, returning with plates of shrimp risotto: so fragrant and delicious that it slipped down easily. Guy was topping up our glasses from a wine bottle nestling in a silver ice-bucket.

The maestro was in command. From a small cooler box he produced a dish of strawberries and a jug of cream. I could feel my cheeks warming. Guy hesitated.

"Do you like strawberries?"

"They're my favourite fruit."

So my fantasy became reality. He held out his hands and I rose and moved towards him. My green top and trousers melted away. We were kneeling on the faux-fur rug in front of the fireplace. Guy fed me a berry or two then placed a cushion behind me; indicating that I should lie down. Then he was kneeling beside me, and hands – his and mine, were unfastening his belt, unzipping his trousers. When he stood up to peel them off, my insides were melting. No thong, but all that mattered was that sensational cock, thrusting from his briefs. All shyness vanished as the hussy that lives inside me unhooked my bra.

Then we were kneeling, facing one another: Guy naked and me wearing just my white knickers. Guy dipped his index finger into the cream and smoothed a dollop on each of my nipples. As he bent his dark head, I felt a million tingles work their way from my breasts down through my stomach – and lower. As he lapped at the cream, his hands were kneading my bottom, pushing down my pants until I wriggled out of them and lay back, my head against the cushion.

He began smoothing cream between my thighs. His fingers, then his lips … then his tongue were working some kind of magic. The soft fur against my bare skin felt decadent … wicked. I looked up at the suit of armour; its visor bland in the candlelight. Could there be someone in there, watching me? The thought excited me and I began to play with my nipples and grind my hips under Guy's probing tongue. He received a double ration of cream.

After the splinters and strobe lights subsided, I saw that Guy was ready for me. I straddled him and sensed his excitement as I fitted myself onto his cock. Empowered, I moved my hips slowly at first then decisively; squeezing him inside me at the end of each stroke. He groaned as I reared up so his tip was almost free, before plunging so he vanished inside me again. He called my name aloud. I thought he was leaving me behind but he reached for the cream and I felt his fingers nudging my tight bud, rhythmically rubbing, helping me climb with him. And all this while he sucked my nipples. Nothing else mattered but this moment. Whether there was anyone inside the armour or not, there was no stopping.

When I rolled off Guy, he cradled me in his arms and kissed the top of my head. The candlelight flickered. What a way to eat dessert. Then his cock seemed to take on a life of its own as it quivered against his thigh. I

71

licked my lips as I reached lazy fingers to caress him. Then someone spoke.

"She is beautiful, like you say to me, Guy. Good evening, Marie."

I sat up, panic making me cover my breasts with my hands. A tall, slender blonde, wearing a crimson satin robe, was walking towards us. I looked at Guy, propped on one elbow beside me. He was smiling lazily at the woman as he beckoned her.

"Just what is going on here?"

"Hush, *ma petite*. Don't fret. This is my wife, Marie."

My fantasy hadn't been designed to accommodate a third person. To be confronted by such a gorgeous female and for the two of us to have the same name was bizarre. I should have grabbed my clothes and got the hell out of there but I was too aflame with desire and curiosity. Marie removed her robe and knelt before us, her lush breasts gleaming in the candle-glow. Guy handed her a vibrator and she began stroking it against herself; Guy watching as he caressed my nipples. He was fondling himself with his other hand. As Marie watched, her breath quickened and I saw that her nipples were erect. Her strokes became more urgent. I reached across and scooped up some cream to splash on top of Guy's rapidly stiffening cock. He began sliding his fingers up and down its length more rapidly, keeping his gaze on Marie's face, while fondling me with his other hand.

Aching, I pushed my fingers inside my own stickiness. Marie was looking straight into my eyes as she screamed, "I'm coming."

The atmosphere was laced with perfume, candle wax and sex. Guy put a second vibrator in my hand. Marie smiled, leaned over and took it. I lay back in Guy's arms while she played me until the rhythm set me writhing. As

72

I began to arch my back, aching for relief, Guy moved on top of me. I groaned as I felt him push inside. Marie was whimpering and writhing as she watched him driving in and out of me. I was so aroused by it all that I came quickly and he was still rock hard when he pulled away and entered Marie from behind. As he eased his length in and out of her, I picked up her vibrator and knelt in front of them, rubbing the tip against her, hoping I'd found the right spot. I guess I must have. Watching those two panting and climaxing in unison made me cry out with them.

Guy gently pushed me on to my side and, as Marie began tonguing my nipples, I couldn't believe I could take any more. But her tongue was warm and wet and velvety and soon I was massaging her while she caressed me. I heard the smack of palm on bum just before I too felt the sharp, sweet sting. We tipped over the edge – our eyes fixed on one another as we shuddered in each other's arms.

"My Maries," I think Guy murmured then.

Soon Marie draped her robe around my shoulders, kissed me on the cheek and showed me upstairs to their private domain. I dressed and came downstairs. Guy took my hands in his and kissed me on each cheek, then on my lips.

"Thank you," he said. "My wife enjoyed meeting you."

It was just as if we had all taken tea together.

"I was worried," I said. "I really thought we'd been caught in the act."

Guy smiled that lazy smile and opened the huge door. Outside a cab was waiting; engine running.

"No, *ma petite*," he said. "She was watching us enjoying each other through a special mirror." I glanced back at the suit of armour. "When she came to join us, I knew that she could wait no longer. You sharing the same name made it even more exciting for her. And for me of course. It is rarely that I close the restaurant in the evening."

He pressed something into my hand as I got into the cab.

Back home, having slept off my jet-lag, I met Tash for a drink.

"So, how were the pensioners?"

"Surprisingly active," I said as we settled ourselves at a table.

"You wish," she chuckled.

I took a photograph from my bag and placed it face down beside her glass.

"Holiday snaps? Where are the rest?"

She turned the photo over. "Marie," she gasped. "Look at the size of … wow, look at you, shagging this gorgeous guy. Who on earth took this?"

"His wife, actually. But I must tell you about Niagara Falls, Tash. You really should go there some time."

# How To Make A Cherry Baby
## by Jade Taylor

I have a thing about oral sex.

I like giving it, love the salty tang of a man's cock on my tongue, love slurping it up like ice cream until he's grabbing my head and moaning my name. I love the loss of control it inspires, the vulnerability of a man placing his precious cock so close to my sharp teeth, love inhaling that scent of lust that comes from burying your face in a man's crotch.

Hell, I even like to swallow.

But the other way round and I'm a little more reluctant.

The *idea* of having a man's head between my legs, his soft mouth on my hard clit, his tongue lapping at my centre drives me wild.

But in reality it doesn't work like that.

I worry.

I worry about the size of my thighs, about the smell of my cunt, about the taste of my arousal.

About whether he's really enjoying himself, or if he's lying there with a mental stop watch thinking that's enough time, I can fuck her now.

And before he knows it instead of pulling his head closer I'm pushing him away.

Usually guys are okay with that, I can come easily enough through sex, and I guess they think it's the destination not the journey that gets you there that counts.

And though occasionally I met a guy who was determined to make me change my mind, none of them even came close.

But then I met Josh.

"I want to make you a Cherry Baby," he tells me, ferreting around in the pantry before coming out with a selection of bottles.

I smile, looking at the clock. "Isn't it a little too early in the day for cocktails?"

He nips at my ear as he walks past me and places the bottles on the work surface. "It's never too early for cocktails."

I laugh, it's not often we have a day off together, and though I know we should be doing housework, or laundry, or mowing the lawn, or any of those hundreds of other jobs, I'm bewitched by this playful mood he's in.

"Besides," he tells me, pouring various drinks into a cocktail shaker. "A Cherry Baby is so much more than just a cocktail."

I'm puzzled now, but say nothing as he shakes the mixture, pouring it into a tall glass full of ice cubes and presenting it to me with a flourish.

"What do you mean?" I ask, but he's says nothing, waiting for me to taste it.

I sip it tentatively.

"Wow, that's got a kick!" I gasp, I love the cherry flavour but it's so strong I put it down, knowing if I drink it too fast it will go straight to my head.

"Nope," he tells me, picking it up and placing it back

76

in my hand. "You have to drink it all down to see what comes next."

His words are light but his eyes are dark with lust and I desperately want to see what comes next.

I drain the glass.

I lean forward to brush my lips against his, and he licks my lips.

"Tastes good, doesn't it? I ask.

"You taste good," he tells me, turning back to his make-shift bar.

Quickly he rustles up another cocktail, and fills my glass once more.

"I don't think I need any more," I tell him, the alcohol already relaxing my body.

"You might do later," he tells me, and taking my hand to lead me back into the dining room, he places it on the nearby window ledge.

He kisses me hard, his tongue in my mouth and his hands on my waist, pulling me close so I can feel his cock hardening against me.

So far I'm enjoying this cocktail.

He moves me backwards, still kissing me, so that the edge of the dining table is against my arse. Then he quickly lifts me on to the table.

It's such a masculine move, to lift me so effortlessly, I'm impressed and turned on.

And also surprised. Although he's not boring in bed, he's never wanted to start anything out of bed before.

And now this definitely looks like he's starting something.

My cunt is wet with excitement as he lays me back on the table and begins unbuttoning my shirt.

"What about the curtains?" I ask, the window is right next to us and though it's rare for anybody to appear at our back door without an invitation, it could still happen.

He ignores me as he finishes opening my blouse, exposing my bra, showing the clearly erect nipples beneath the thin lace.

It's no use even pretending that I'm not enjoying this with my body betraying me so blatantly.

Then he moves down to the bottom of the table and moves my legs so I'm lying with my knees up and legs apart. He pulls up my skirt, leaving the material bunched around my waist, and goes to pull down my panties.

I try to sit up, try to reach for his hands, try to tell him to stop. Having the neighbours catch me with my bra on display is nothing, having them pop round and seem my exposed vulva is different.

"No," he tells me, holding my hands tight. He moves back around the table and moves my left hand to grip the left side, and my right hand to grip the right side. "You have to keep your hands there if you want to learn how to make a Cherry Baby."

I want to tell him no, to say we should move this upstairs, but instead I grip the table.

He's never shown any signs of dominance before but now as he's telling me what to do I'm so turned on my breathing is getting harder before he's even touched me.

I have a feeling gripping on to the table's a good idea, that I'm going to need a tight grip before long.

He taps my bottom and I lift it for him without a word, letting him slowly inch down my panties, letting out a little moan as I feel some of my wetness come off them and rub against my thighs.

I can't believe I'm so exposed, and it feels even more erotic that my skirt and blouse are still on when my cunt is so on display. I can feel myself getting slick and swollen, and wonder if he can see, before realising with the sunlight streaming in and the position I'm in, *of course* he can see.

And he likes it.

"God, you're turned on," Josh says, lowering his head as if to inhale the scent of me. For a moment I stiffen, sure he's going to try and lick me, but he quickly moves away.

Instead he reaches into his back pocket and pulls out a bottle I hadn't noticed earlier.

"This is step two in how to make a Cherry Baby," he tells me, and I see what it is.

Cherry flavoured lubricant.

He moves around the table once more as he begins pouring it across my neck, my shoulders, and my breasts. I don't know where he's been storing it, but it's cold, and I gasp as it touches my skin, as it drips on my nipples and they instantly pucker up.

Then his hot mouth is warming me as he slowly begins to lick it off. He starts at my neck and my collarbone, one of my most sensitive spots, and I shiver as his tongue touches me, sighing loudly. His tongue delves further down, licking my stomach and inside my belly button where the lube has pooled, and I begin to moan.

Then his mouth moves up to my breasts and even though I'm still wearing my bra, I can feel the liquid through the flimsy material and can feel his tongue licking me clean. Even through the bra I feel his tongue swirl around my nipples, and as his teeth begin to graze at my tender flesh I grip the table hard.

My breasts feel more sensitive in my damp bra than they do when naked, and I know my juices are flowing out of me as quickly as the moans that keep escaping my mouth.

My nipples feel connected to my clit, and as he continues licking at them I can feel the cool air around my bare arse, my bare vulva, my clit so eager for attention. I can feel the glass of the table cool against my ass, and wonder if when I move I'll leave a slick trail of my arousal.

I certainly feel wet enough.

"You like that?" he asks, as if there could be any doubt.

I can only nod dumbly, my voice far too shaky to form words.

"Then we'll move on to step three."

He vanishes briefly into the kitchen, and though I'm still blatantly exposed and now covered in sticky cherry lube, I can't move, wanting to see what comes next.

He comes back in carrying a punnet of cherries.

"I love cherries," he tells me as he moves to the bottom of the table. "But you have to be really careful if there's still stones in."

He holds one between his finger and thumb, rolling it around as if testing it.

I want him touching something else.

"You have to nibble at it really soft and slow to get to all that juicy flesh," he tells me, and I wonder where he's going with this.

I don't have to wonder for long.

He moves a chair to the edge of the table at sits at it, so he is looking directly at my cunt.

He reaches forward and carefully places the cherry between my swollen lips.

"Oh," I gasp, both shocked and excited.

He reaches for another.

Now as he places it between my lips he rubs it softly against my clit first.

"Oh God," I exclaim.

I can't believe what's happening as he reaches for another, rubbing it harder against my clit, then another, and another.

I now have my inner lips pushed rudely apart, full of cherries, and all I can think of how fucking horny this is.

"But what I really like is when cherries are really juicy," he tells me, pouring lube over my already slick cunt, making me gasp and making my cunt tighten as if trying to hold all those lovely cherries in place.

"Now," Josh tells me, as he moves closer to me, "I know you don't like oral, so I promise I won't lick you unless you ask me."

And then he starts eating the cherries.

At first he licks them, and though his tongue isn't touching me, the sensation of those slick cherries rolling around against me are driving me wild, and I'm gripping the table so tight my knuckles ache. Every time one moves against my clit I cry out, and it just makes Josh lick at them harder.

Then he begins nibbling at their flesh. I can feel his mouth getting closer to my flesh, feel the cherry juice bursting against my sensitive skin, can feel the roughness of the stones starting to show through.

I can't believe I'm letting him do this.

My hands are gripping the table so hard I'm sure I'm going to break it, my breath is coming too hard and too fast and my knees are shaking hard, but I still can't stop.

I can't believe that I've let him put me on this table and expose me so completely (the drink was strong, but not that strong!), that the curtains are open and I'm semi-naked when anyone could turn up, that I've let him conquer my inhibitions so completely with some lube and some fruit.

81

I can't believe the sensations that are flooding through my body, how my skin feels so hot and tight, my nipples so hard, and my cunt as if it's about to explode, ready to shoot out those cherry stones like fireworks.

And I can't believe what I'm about to say.

"Please lick me," I ask him.

He moves his hands to pull my lips apart even further and I feel the cherries slowly roll out of me.

Then he licks me.

And it's enough.

His tongue touches my clit and it's like I'm melting.

I grab his head.

He licks my clit and I implode, my orgasm shaking me hard I'm gasping and shuddering and holding on to the table for dear life as rivers of heat flow through me and waves of pleasure engulf me.

I'm all lazy pleasure and easy malleability as my knees finally lower and he grabs my hips to pull me closer to the edge of the table.

"I'm not going to last long," he tells me as he quickly sheathes his cock in latex and thrusts inside me.

"That's not a problem," I tell him as his thumb softly circles my clit.

I'm so spent I can barely move as he pumps inside me, but he doesn't complain as he grabs my hips once more to thrust into me more deeply.

His thumb moves more quickly, and though I wouldn't have thought it possible, I can feel another orgasm approaching.

This time when I come hard, he is with me, and as he judders inside me he calls my name as I call his.

I see stars and smell cherries.

"And this is step four," he says when we've finally recovered, beginning to untangle limbs and pull apart our sticky bodies.

"There's a step four?" I ask, amazed; how could there be a step four?

He passes me a flimsy parcel wrapped in black tissue paper.

"I know how shy you are about … this, so I thought these might help."

I open the parcel.

Inside are some gorgeous frilly white panties, decorated with bright red cherries.

"I thought that maybe if you were too shy to ask, then you could just wear these, and I'd know exactly what you wanted."

I kissed him hard, not caring that he tasted of me.

I love the panties.

And that's how I finally got over my aversion to receiving oral sex.

And that's how you make a Cherry Baby.

# First Name Terms
## by Roxanne Sinclair

Grace lifted the mug of coffee to her mouth, pouted her peony-coloured lips and blew over its surface. As her gentle breath rippled the liquid her eyes looked straight ahead at the man standing less than ten feet away.

Mr Barlow.

Grace wondered if he would let her call him Edward.

She smiled as she rested the mug on her lower lip to allow some of the hot liquid to enter her mouth.

He had no idea what was coming his way.

As soon as Grace had heard that Steve Barnes had left the company and they were going to promote from within she'd known that she wanted the job, must have the job.

And she knew just the way to get it.

He wouldn't know what had hit him.

She was still smiling to herself when he turned around and saw her watching him. She dropped her eyelashes demurely like the virgin she hadn't been for about fifteen years. When she lifted them again she saw that he was still looking at her.

"Hello, Mr Barlow," she said.

"Miss Lloyd," he replied with a smile on his lips and a look of admiration on his face.

It only took the few seconds that their eyes were

84

locked for her to know that he was going to be putty in her hands.

Later she stopped his secretary on her way to the coffee machine.

"I'll get it for him," Grace said. "I'm getting one for myself anyway."

"Oh thanks, Grace, he's milk no sugar."

A couple of minutes later she lowered the mug onto his desk, leaning forward just enough to offer him a glimpse of her cleavage.

"Milk no sugar," Grace said with a sideways glance.

"Just the way I like it," he replied with a glance of his own.

"I aim to please," she rested her hands on the desk and used her arms to push her breasts together, deepening the cleavage on show.

She stayed like that for a couple of seconds locking eyes with him all the time.

"Thank you."

Grace pushed herself up from his desk. She walked away with a look of satisfaction on her face and the knowledge that her arse, barely contained within a skirt that finished at the very top of her thigh, looked great. She exaggerated her sway just in case he hadn't noticed.

She could feel his eyes on her all the way.

Without breaking stride she looked at the clock on the wall opposite. In a couple of hours people would start to leave for the day. Mr Barlow was always the last to leave but tonight they would be leaving together.

Grace watched each of her colleagues leave making the excuse that she was, "Just finishing something", every time anyone asked if she was leaving.

Eventually they were the only people left. But neither of them was working. Both were pretending to be busy but the only thing either of them was doing was observing the other.

After a while Grace gave up with the pretence and walked towards his office carrying the thing that she was "just finishing".

His head was down but she knew that he was watching her.

She paused in the doorway and leaned against its frame. She tapped on the glass door.

He looked up, pretending to be surprised.

"Grace," he said, "you're here late. I didn't realise that there was anyone still here."

Like hell you didn't, Grace thought. But she kept the thought to herself and said, "I just wanted to finish this." She held a sheaf of papers in her hand.

When he said, "You'd better give me what you've got," she knew that her plan was right on track.

She flicked the wedge from under the door with her toe and it closed behind her as she walked into the room.

His eyes moved up and down her length as she walked the half dozen steps to his desk. From the look on his face Grace could tell that he wouldn't be playing hard to get.

She walked over to him and perched herself on the edge of his desk. He pushed his chair back at an angle and admired her legs. Grace knew that they were good, she'd worn the skirt especially to show them off at their best. It was clear that the effort had not been in vain.

She handed him the papers and he tossed them onto the desk without looking at them.

Grace dropped her head onto her chest and looked at the bulge that had formed in his crotch. His trousers couldn't hide what was happening there.

He looked at it too and laughed, "Getting a bit tight in

there."

Grace bent over and rubbed her hand over the mound and he wriggled in his seat. She gripped the zip between her fingers and pulled gently. After a slight resistance the zip made its way down its tracks. With a practised hand she reached inside, located the hole in the front of his boxer shorts and released the beast within.

"That's better," she said with her eyes still on the throbbing length of cock that she had released.

He slid his chair forward and moved his hand onto her thigh. He stroked it a few times before allowing his fingertips to move towards what lay beyond.

He found her own mound encased in lace and he stroked her through the fabric. Slowly he found the edge of the garment and forced his fingers under it, finding her shaven and soft.

"Unless you want those ripping," he said, "you'd better take them off."

She appeared to consider her options for a second before pushing herself off the edge of the desk. She stood before him and lifted her skirt over her hips. She let him look at her a while, knowing that the lace barely covered her at all. With her fingers stiff and straight she pushed her hand into the front of her knickers. She could feel her excitement in the dampness that she found there. He could hear it in the noise she made. When she removed her hand she offered it to him and he took her fingers in his mouth and licked her juices from them.

"Tasty," he said.

She looped her thumbs over the edges of her panties and gave them a gentle tug. She lowered them to her knees and then allowed them to fall to her ankles. She kicked them aside.

"Why don't you take that skirt off too," his voice had

taken on a hoarse quality.

"Why don't you," her voice was playful.

He didn't need inviting twice and pushed himself to his feet. He came towards her with his cock twitching at a forty-five degree angle. He found the zip where it rested on her hip and opened it. Seconds later the skirt was where her knickers had been and she kicked it away in the same manner.

He grabbed her arse and pulled her into him so that his rod was pressed against her naked crotch.

With their faces inches apart she took his tie between her fingers and loosened it. She could feel his breath on her face and sensed its increasing speed. He moved in to kiss her but she pulled back.

"Patience, Mr Barlow," she giggled.

Their hands became a frenzy of movement, opening buttons and removing clothes. Soon the only garment left between them was a bra that matched the knickers that Grace had already cast aside.

He stroked the soft curve of her breasts before his fingers followed the path of the straps up to her shoulder and down the back. He freed each hook in turn and caught the bra as it fell from Grace's shoulders. He tossed it away.

Grace stood naked in her boss's glass-walled office with her equally naked boss and she was more aroused than she had ever been before. She had also never felt more in control. She knew that he would do whatever she asked him to.

Grace turned around and leaned over the desk and, with a sweep of her hand, cleared a space. Then she waited for a moment to see what he would do.

She wasn't surprised when she felt his end trying to burrow its way between her legs. He leaned his chest against her back and wrapped his arms around her cupping a breast in each hand. As he kneaded them he planted kisses on the back of her neck.

He released her breasts and moved his hands down her body. They moved over her stomach and towards the V at the top of her legs.

He found her as soft as he was hard, and not completely shaven. He found the contrast between smooth skin and the line of soft down irresistible and he moved his finger from one to the other.

On the fourth sweep of the area he stopped on the line that ran down her crack. He moved his finger from side to side until the slit opened and he made his way in.

She tingled under his touch and inched her legs apart to afford him easier access, allowing him to rub her until she was almost ready to explode before grabbing his hand.

"What?" It was a sound more than a word.

"I want to see you when you fuck me," Grace explained as she turned around.

"Do you want me to fuck you?"

"Oh yes please, Mr Barlow. I would very much like you to fuck me." She spoke the words slowly in a voice just above a whisper.

"Then you'd better open up."

"Anything you say, Mr Barlow," she said, laying back and taking the weight on her elbows. She lifted her feet, balanced her heels on the edge of the desk and allowed her knees to fall to the sides.

"You are very beautiful," he said staring at her pussy.

She liked the way that she felt as she lay exposed before him. She shifted her weight onto her left elbow, freeing her right hand to move down to her crotch and spread her lips in invitation. Once again it was the only invitation he needed and he took his enlarged cock in his hand and moved it to the rim of her hole.

He paused a second before forcing himself forward. His excitement had made him large but hers had made her wet and he entered her smoothly.

Once he was all the way in he paused for just a second before withdrawing almost all the way. He then grabbed hold of her thighs and used them to pull himself back into her with even greater force, He took four or five thrusts to find his rhythm but once he'd got it right he hit the spot every time.

Grace lay back and enjoyed the ride.

She uttered a little cry each time he entered her which he took as encouragement to go harder and faster.

Soon those little cries had become something bordering on screams.

Then without realising it had happened, her ankles were around his neck and her hips were off the desk. She moved her hands to her tits and squeezed, gently at first but as her excitement grew her movements grew harder until she dug her fingernails into the soft flesh as her orgasm washed over her.

She felt him grow inside her just before his warm jet told her that he was spent.

They moved around each other searching for various pieces of clothing and dressed in silence. As he fastened the buttons of his shirt his eyes glanced at the sheets of paper that Grace had given him.

He gave her CV a cursory glance.

"You're hired," he said as he reached for his jacket.

"Why thank you, Mr Barlow," she said coyly.

"Oh please," he said, turning the light out with one hand and feeling her backside with the other. "Call me Ed."

# Merrilee Gets Her Own Way
## by Eleanor Powell

She tossed the skirt and top onto the growing pile of rejected clothes on her bed. She knew she wanted to look just right for him, sexy yes, but not cheap.

Rummaging through her wardrobe for the umpteenth time – Ah! Now she thought, I'd forgotten I had this. She stepped into the dress and fastened the buttons down the front. Then looking at her reflection in the full-length mirror – yes that's it, she told herself.

The green dress matched her eyes perfectly, contrasting so beautifully with her auburn hair. She was showing some cleavage, enough to be a teaser but not too much.

It was a bright sunny day as she set off to go to town. It wasn't far so the walk would do her good. She was gratified to hear a low wolf whistle as she passed a building site. Knowing she looked sexy – a smile lit up her face. Normally she would have been flattered at this male attention – she might even have stopped to flirt, but now she had her mind on only one thing – she was a woman with a mission.

She looked up apprehensively at the darkening sky; grey clouds had replaced the white fluffy ones of only a moment ago. A large raindrop landed on her nose, then another and another.

Not now please, she pleaded with the gods of the weather.

Unable to see any shelter she had no choice but to keep going – hoping that this was just a passing shower.

People were hurrying by crouching under their umbrellas paying no attention to the small auburn haired young woman, looking wet and bedraggled as she entered 'The Sex Boutique'.

I must look a right mess, she thought. After all the trouble I took getting dressed. I did so want to look my best.

The shop was empty except for a gorgeous hunk standing behind the counter. Merrilee got the familiar butterflies in her tummy at the sight of him. Oh how she wished he'd put her over his knee and give her a long sensuous spanking, just the thought of it made her bottom tingle and her pussy juice up.

But geez there's not much chance of that now, she thought. Why did it have to rain and spoil my plans?

'Oh! hello, Merrilee, good to see you again,' said Joe the manager of the shop. 'Did you go swimming and forget to take your towel?'

'No,' she retorted. 'I went to feed the ducks and fell in.'

'Now, Merrilee, there's no need to be sarcastic,' Joe said, laughing at her obvious discomfiture.

'Right we can't have you dripping all over the shop now, can we? Come on in the back and get dried.' Joe ushered her into the room behind the shop.

He turned on the gas fire. 'We'll soon get you warm.'

Although it was a warm day, Merrilee realised she had goose bumps and her teeth were chattering.

Joe disappeared into another room and came back

with a huge towel.

'Here, Merrilee, take off those wet clothes, they'll be dry in no time,' he said.

'But what if someone comes in, I've only got my bra and pants under this dress?'

'Don't worry, no one can see you. Put the towel around you, if you're modest. Well I am expecting someone anytime now. I think he'd like to meet you.'

'Who is it?' she asked.

'His name's Jed, now come on, get out of those wet clothes.

'That's a good girl,' Joe said as she stepped out of her dress.

He draped it over a chair.

'It should be dry in no time.'

Merrilee wrapped the towel around herself, then realising that was not the image she wanted to portray, tossed it aside.

She was aware of Joe's admiring grey eyes looking her up and down. She knew she looked good in her black Wonderbra with matching briefs.

Having towel-dried her auburn hair she asked Joe for the use of a comb. 'Don't want it drying any which way,' she said.

By now Merrilee's mind was spinning. Here was her golden opportunity. She so wanted Joe to spank her. Maybe she could turn things around and get what she wanted after all. She smiled mischievously at the thought.

Joe couldn't take his eyes off her. 'Now, Merrilee, that was a cheeky smile just then. What were you thinking?'

'Nothing,' and she started wandering around the room – picking up various leather items, examining them and putting them down again. 'Hey! what's this?'

'That Merrilee is a flogger. Haven't you seen one before?'

'What do you do with it?' she asked, looking wide-eyed and innocent.

'Shall I show you?'

'Hmmm, maybe, or there again, maybe not,' she shrugged her shoulders.

'Merrilee, little girls who can't make up their own minds – may find themselves having their minds made up for them.'

'What do you mean?'

'I'm going to give you the spanking you so richly deserve.'

'Yeah, right, it takes a man not a mouse.'

'Now that sounds like a challenge to me,' said Joe, as he moved towards her.

She backed away from him until she felt the cold metal of a filing cabinet pressing into her back.

'Come on, Merrilee, you've been a little brat for months now, it's high time you learned not to be a tease.' Catching hold of her wrist, Joe pulled her across the room. Sitting down on the couch he pulled her over his knee.

'Don't you dare touch me,' she said … sending a prayer of thanks up to the spanking gods.

'You, young lady, are not in a position to tell me what I can or can't do.' Joe brought his right hand down on her upturned bottom – leaving a burning sensation in her right cheek. Raising his arm he brought his hand down again on her left one.

'Owwwww! That bloody hurt, you lousy rotten sod.'

'Swearing at me, Merrilee, is not one of your best ideas,' Joe said. 'And a spanking is meant to hurt.'

She wriggled but he just held her even tighter. Oh how

she loved a masterful man.

'This is not a proper spanking, Merrilee, a proper spanking is on the bare bottom.'

Joe hooked his fingers into the waistband of her knickers and pulled them down to mid thigh.

Merrilee reached behind her and attempted to pull them back up again.

'No you don't, young lady.'

He caught hold of her right arm and held it up her back.

'This is what all brats should be getting on a regular basis.'

He went on spanking her bare bottom … first one cheek then the other.

She increased her wriggling as her bottom started to tingle and feel very warm.

'Your bottom is definitely looking much better now,' he gave a grunt of satisfaction. 'But it's not nearly red enough.'

'You lousy rotten swine,' she squealed while thumping his legs.

'Thump me again brat and I'll take my belt off to you.'

Merrilee thought about this new threat for the whole of a second – then she thumped his leg again.

Joe pulled her up into a sitting position. She watched totally enthralled as he slowly pulled his leather belt from its loops. Her eyes growing bigger as he wrapped the belt around his hand, leaving about twelve inches.

'Right, young lady, let's have you back over my knee, maybe a taste of my belt will improve your behaviour.' He pulled her back over his knee. Jiggled her about until he was satisfied she was in the right position and raised his right hand and arm …

The shrill screaming of the shop bell made them both jump.

'That may be Jed.' Pulling her up unceremoniously into a sitting position he handed her a vibrator from the shelf.

'Here Merrilee enjoy yourself,' he left her and went through to the shop closing the door behind him.

Merrilee's pussy was by now hot and throbbing, her juices flowing – she was so wet. The vibrator slipped inside her easily – she lay back on the couch, pushing it in and out going ever deeper into her pussy, she was breathing erratically, almost gasping for breath; her green eyes were closed, she just knew she was going to come – she was so absorbed in what she was doing, she didn't realise she was no longer alone.

Joe had returned, but he had someone with him.

'Hello, Merrilee,' said this deep masculine voice. 'I was hoping to meet you. Joe has told me all about your brattiness.'

'Not me, I'm a little angel.'

'Of course you are, but even angels need reminding every so often that their halos are slipping. Isn't that right, Joe?'

'With you all the way, mate.'

'Seems I obviously interrupted something, I take it you were spanking her? So why don't you start again, Joe? I'd love to watch.'

'With pleasure, Jed. Hey, why don't you video it? Would you like that, Merrilee? Jed makes spanking videos.'

'Yes, yes, yes,' squealed Merrilee excitedly. 'I've always wanted to be in a video.'

'Good girl,' said Joe approvingly.

'That's the second time you called me a good girl.

Told you I was.'

'You, Merrilee, are good at being naughty.'

'I've got my camcorder in the car, won't be a minute,' Jed left the shop.

He came back carrying his camcorder and a Tripod. 'Joe you better shut up shop now,' he suggested.

With the shop closed and Jed's camcorder set up, Merrilee asked if she could freshen up a bit. Taking her dress that was dry by then, she went into the washroom.

Eventually, all was in place.

It was decided that Joe should do the spanking, as Jed was the expert with the camcorder.

'Merrilee, sit down on the couch, you, Joe, sit next to her,' said Jed. 'Now Merrilee, I want you to do what comes naturally to you, be a brat and you Joe sort her out with a sound spanking. OK?'

'Absolutely, there's nothing I'd like better,' said Joe.

'Oh, and, Merrilee, forget about the camera – just enjoy yourself.'

She felt giddy with excitement, wasn't this just what she'd been dreaming about for ever.

Joe interrupted her thoughts. 'Now Merrilee get back over my knee,'

'Shan't,' she said. 'You can't make me.'

Joe gave a big sigh, 'Seems to me you need some persuasion.' Getting hold of her left arm, he yanked her over his knee.

His left arm encircled her waist, while her short tight skirt had ridden up – revealing her cute little bottom covered by black see-through knickers.

She wriggled, trying to escape as he raised his right arm and brought the palm of his hand down on her right cheek. Raising his arm again, his hard hand landed on her left cheek.

'Yeowwwww!' she shrieked. 'That bloody hurt.'

'Swearing, Merrilee, tut tut most unladylike.'

Joe landed another twenty spanks on her upturned bottom cheeks.

Despite her wriggling, she couldn't escape the hot stinging blows. She felt his hard cock pressing into her side. Great, she thought, he's getting turned on too.

'I think these knickers need to come down,' Joe said. 'I don't think you can feel this spanking through them.' He tugged her panties down her thighs.

'That's better, I can see what I'm doing now.' He continued spanking her.

Merrilee, through the stinging of her bottom, also felt that old familiar feeling of excitement. Her bottom tingled and felt as if it was on fire. 'Oh my God!' she cried out as her wildly kicking legs allowed the floodwaters to open and her juices ran freely.

'Merrilee, you naughty little girl, you are soaking my trousers, have you no shame?'

She giggled, wriggling her bottom provocatively at him.

'It seems, you little brat, that my hand is having no effect on you. Maybe my belt will get through to you better.'

Joe pulled her into a sitting position and she watched excitedly as he slowly removed his belt from its loops. He wound the belt around his hand – leaving enough to use on her bottom. Then taking hold of her wrist he once again pulled her over his knee.

Merrilee had a feeling of satisfaction. She loved the belt and now here she was getting her own way. Was this really happening to her or was she having a lovely dream and would wake up to find herself alone in her bed?

'I don't like the belt,' she protested. And to prove it

she soaked his trousers even more.

'That's OK, Merrilee,' laughed Joe. 'You're not supposed to like it. You're being punished for being a brat.'

'My bottom's on fire.' She renewed her struggles. But the more she wriggled the tighter he held her.

'You're making a lot of fuss, your bottom is only slightly pink.' Joe pulled her up once more into a sitting position. 'Let's try something new.'

Joe pushed her over the arm of the couch. 'Come on, get that bottom of yours up higher.' And he pushed her head down into the seat of the couch.

'Now stay there,' he ordered.

She didn't usually do as she was told and had no intention of doing so now.

She stood up, but Joe was across the room in a couple of strides; pushing her back down over the arm of the couch. Giving her another dozen hard stinging slaps with his hand, causing her to violently wriggle her bottom.

'Now maybe you will stay down,' he said.

This time she did as she was told. But twisting her head she tried to see what he was up to.

But whatever it was he was hiding behind his back, she couldn't see.

Pushing her head back down into the seat of the couch – she felt something soft but slightly stingy land on her bottom and whatever it was wrapped around her hips.

What on earth was it? she thought. It was a new sensation but wow! It was fantastic. 'What are you using?' she asked.

'The flogger, Merrilee, you asked me earlier how it was used. Now you are about to find out.'

'Hey! I love it. It … it,' she had difficulty explaining how it made her feel.

99

'It is meant to titillate rather than hurt,' explained Joe. 'Now if it's OK with you, Merrilee, I'll carry on.'

'Well stop talking about it and get on with it then.'

'You, young lady, have far too much to say for yourself.'

He raised his right arm and brought the flogger down on her bottom.

She couldn't understand why there seemed to be a pause between each stroke. So she twisted her head again to watch what he was doing. He was straightening out the fronds of the flogger and twisting them before he aimed another blow at her bottom.

After a few more strokes she was wriggling about again – but now it was because she was getting so aroused and was moaning softly.

Suddenly Joe stopped hitting her and instead he gently nudged her legs apart and let the fronds of the flogger trail between her legs.

'You're turning me on,' she hissed.

'Shall I stop then?'

'Oh God, no,' she gasped.

Joe continued hitting her with it, then every so often, letting the fronds of soft suede gently caress the inside of her thighs.

Without warning the rhythm changed. Now he was using the flogger to flail gently between her shoulder blades; using a circular movement.

Joe's use of the flogger had Merrilee wanting more and more. He would start at her shoulder blades and slowly work his way down her back to her violently swaying bottom. Then he would tease her until she was almost screaming out for release.

He stopped hitting her with the flogger.

She soon knew his intention as she felt him enter her

from behind. As he thrust into her, she pushed her hot twitching bottom up to meet him.

She came first, closely followed by Joe. But as his cum filled her, she orgasmed again. It came in waves, ebbing and flowing for some minutes.

They were both exhausted. Sitting on the couch with their arms around each other, they'd have fallen asleep if Jed hadn't spoken.

'Well done, you two. I think we have a new spanking video star Joe. Would you like that, Merrilee, to be a professional actor and get paid for being spanked?'

'I wouldn't like it Jed ... I'd love it,' laughed Merrilee.

# Tour De Frances
## by J. Manx

It was my friend Annie who put me on to it.

'Come on, Frances, why don't you give it a try, you could lose some weight.'

'You cheeky cow.'

'No, seriously, there are some fit blokes there, I promise you.'

She was right, I could lose a few pounds but the suggestion of some interesting men was the more telling pull. So, on a Saturday morning, I turned up with Annie at the local cycling club. There were only four women but about fifteen blokes. A good ratio, and the men all looked fit, lean and lithe. Annie introduced me to a few of them. They were polite, attentive and likeable. I'd already made up my mind … I liked cycling.

There was one man I noticed. He was talking to two other women and, although I couldn't tell what they were saying, I knew by their body language that they were flirting outrageously. He was good-looking and he knew it. Yeah, I thought , he's an arrogant sod. But I couldn't stop my eyes being drawn towards him. I was a little irritated that, out of all the men there, he was the only one who hadn't even looked in my direction.

A little later, an older guy told us all to mount up. He

put us into groups for twenty, ten and five mile distances. Annie and I were the only two in the five mile group. I felt a little inadequate, although, if truth be told, I wasn't sure that five miles wouldn't kill me. 'Don't worry, girls,' said the older guy, 'a few weeks and you'll be up to the ten mile runs.' He turned and shouted to Mr Arrogant. 'Hey, Peter, are you going to keep an eye on these today?'

Peter nodded, looked at me and smiled. Who does he think he is? I thought, but my heart was racing.

We all started off at the same time but soon lost the others as they moved ahead. Embarrassingly, Annie too pulled away from me, having kindly stayed back for the first half mile. I was far too slow.

'No, go on,' I shouted, 'you go ahead, I'll be fine.'

It wasn't long before I was totally alone, puffing away and feeling a little silly. Then Mr Arrogant turns up.

'Hi, getting a bit difficult?' he smiled.

'No, I'm fine, just haven't been cycling for years.'

'That's the spirit, keep it up.'

He fell in behind me and began chatting away. All I could think about was how I must look from behind. But after a while I found myself chatting back to him, he wasn't arrogant at all. We got back well before the others.

'Better take it easy for the first few times, ease yourself into it,' said Peter as he parked his bike against a wall.

I felt a little bit mean about my earlier judgment. 'I hope I haven't ruined your ride?'

'No, I went out earlier today, I've already done my 30 miles.'

'I must say you look incredibly fit.' Was I flirting?

'I love being out in the open,' he said. 'I love the fresh

103

air and there's some beautiful countryside around here. If you're serious about cycling, I'd love to show you some of the routes. We could take it easy at first, build up slowly?'

'I'd like that,' I said , trying not to sound too enthusiastic.

Peter smiled. 'OK, then. What about tomorrow morning? Weather looks good.'

'That'd be great.'

I normally have a lie in on Sunday mornings but I wasn't about to miss an opportunity like this. I told Annie on the way home.

'I'd be careful,' she said, 'he'll try it on with you given half a chance. He's only after one thing.'

'Thanks,' I said, 'I'll remember that.' Great, I thought.


The following morning, I took a bit more care over my appearance. We'd arranged to meet at the club. I got there first and watched as Peter rode up on his racing bike. He was a superb specimen. He was tanned, wearing black lycra cycling shorts and a yellow lycra top. They looked as though they'd been sprayed on and accentuated his muscled thighs. He pulled up beside me, smiling.

'You're looking good, all ready for a long ride?' He had a twinkle in his eye.

'I'll do my best,' I said. 'I'm a little stiff from yesterday. I don't suppose you get stiff too often?'

Peter laughed. He got off his bike and lay it on the ground.

'Here,' he said, coming up behind me, 'let's make sure your saddle's the right height and you're properly balanced.'

He stood astride the back wheel and leaned over my back, his arms extended over mine, his hands covering mine on the handlebars. His deep voice was soft in my ear as he explained the correct posture and a few other things. But I wasn't listening. I'd gone into a kind of daze, acutely aware of his arms and body around me. I wanted him to fuck me. I was disappointed when he pulled away.

'Come on then, let's get started.'

He got on his bike. 'Remember,' he said, a wicked look in his eye, 'it's just a matter of rhythm, all riding's about rhythm. Once we get the rhythm right everything will come easily and you'll feel like riding for ever.' He laughed.

Stop playing with me, I thought, please, you can have me anytime.

'OK,' he said, mounting his bike, 'Let's get out to the countryside, it's a beautiful day.'

And it was, a warm, clear skied, fresh, spring day.

I followed Peter. After several miles we'd left the town behind and were in open countryside. The views were beautiful, particularly the one in front of me. Every so often, Peter would raise his bottom from the saddle in order to get a bit more power up a hill. From my vantage point I could see the 'V' of his back, narrowing from his broad shoulders to his narrow hips, and a cute, firm bottom bobbing up and down. Lucky old bike, I thought.

During a particularly arduous hill climb, Peter looked back over his shoulder at me. 'Just up the top of the hill and we'll stop for a break.' At the top of the hill he was waiting for me. Despite using the lowest gear, I'd had to dismount halfway up the hill and walk the rest of the way. Peter met me, smiling. 'You've done really well,' he said, and I felt rather proud of myself. He locked up the bikes, took me by the hand and he led me, on a pathway, through some trees. There was a beautiful smell of spring in the air, the greenery and blossom adding a faint perfume to the freshness. The canopy of trees had darkened and cooled the track that we walked along. We didn't speak. I was enjoying the physical contact, my hand in his, and the surrounding silence. After a short distance we broke through the trees and the effect was exhilarating. We were at the top of a hill and stretching out in front of us were miles of unspoilt countryside, resting beneath a blue sky.

'Wow, that's beautiful,' I exclaimed. Peter, who was still holding my hand, pulled me close to him and put his arm around my shoulder. We stood for about a minute, just taking in the view. My heart was thumping. I'd responded by putting my arm around his waist. I slipped my hand down and rested it on his bottom. I was feeling as randy as hell. Peter turned and kissed me. It was a long, sensuous kiss. He broke away.

'Lift up your arms.'

I did as I was told. He pulled my tennis shirt over my head, reached around and unclasped my bra. 'Wow,' he said, 'what lovely breasts, perfect nipples.' He reached out and, with both hands, gently caressed and squeezed my nipples. I felt pulses of pleasure.

'Oh, that feels wonderful, don't stop.'

He continued for a while then bent his head down and began to lick and suck my breasts. Now, fully aroused, I broke away and took off the remainder of my clothes, wriggling sensuously as I removed my track suit bottoms. Naked, I put my arms back around his neck and we kissed. This time the kissing was more urgent. Peter ran his hands up and down my back. He caressed and squeezed my bottom. Again, I broke away.

'Come on, your turn to strip off.'

Peter crossed his arms and pulled his lycra top over

his head. I stepped back and let out an appreciative sigh before stepping forward and running my hands over his chest and shoulders. We began kissing again. The soft breeze felt like another pair of hands caressing me. I broke away, knelt down and peeled his tight lycra shorts down over his thighs. His cock, like a bent sapling, sprang out in front of me.

'God,' I laughed, 'this spring air certainly helps things grow.'

He didn't respond but looked at me, expectantly. I didn't disappoint. I ran my tongue slowly up and down the length of his cock, stopping occasionally at the base to take his balls in my mouth. I gently sucked them while I caressed the head of his cock with one hand and stroked a muscled thigh with the other. I then gripped both thighs and took the end of his cock into my mouth and delicately massaged the tip with my lips and tongue. Peter was now holding my head in his hands and letting out short gasps of breath. I took my mouth from his cock, admiring the purple head which was now glistening from the reflected sunlight. I gripped it with both hands and looked up at him.

'So, what about this riding lesson you were going to give me?'

I stood up, walked several paces away from him, found a thickly grassed area and got down on all fours.

'Now then,' I said, 'if I remember rightly, this is the correct riding position.'

I stretched my elbows in front of me, so that my face was almost touching the floor, then I raised my bottom high in the air and wiggled it seductively.

'Is this the right way?' I said, innocently. I'd never felt so randy. I got no verbal reply but felt hands gripping my hips and we both gasped as his cock filled me. He began to fuck me slowly and I felt his hands caressing my bottom and thighs. I looked ahead of me and felt a tremendous sense of liberation. Here I was, stark naked, in beautiful, open countryside, the warm sun on my body, a soft breeze caressing me and a beautiful man fucking me. I began to moan, then shout, the noise fading into the distance. At first, I moved rhythmically with him but as his thrusts became more urgent and powerful I leaned forward, stretching out my arms and gripping handfuls of grass to stabilise myself. I rested my head on the ground, taking in the fragrance of the grass as I felt strong waves of pleasure wash over me. I felt Peter's grip tighten around my hips as he, too, reached orgasm. Afterwards, we cuddled on the soft grass for a while before getting dressed. I was thankful that the journey back was mostly downhill, I felt knackered.

Peter confided in me several days later. 'I've been cycling for years and that's the first time I've ever made love in the open.'

I didn't believe him, but he was adamant. Anyway, he says he's determined to develop this new aspect of the sport and I'm determined to help him. We've already fucked in several well known beauty spots. We call it 'Faffing about' (Fresh Air Fucking). Annie asked me recently whether I was going on holiday this year.

'Yeah, I'm going cycling with Peter.'

'Anywhere in particular?'

'Not really, we're just cycling from place to place, see where we end up. You know, just generally faffing about.'

She didn't seem that interested.

P.S. I've lost half a stone and I'm as fit as a fiddle. I'm

not sure whether it's the cycling or the Faffing.

# He Fucked/She Fucked
## by Landon Dixon

Skylar gripped my stiff cock at the base, stretched her obscenely long tongue down to her hand and then licked all the way up my throbbing shaft, slow and sloppy-wet and almost in a straight line. I shivered, and groaned. The busty party girl then swung her tongue around my mushroomed cockhead, setting my whole body to vibrating. She slid her smeared lips over the top of my bloated knob and sucked on it, and I thought for sure I'd lose it; that the whole wild, crazy experiment to inject some new life and positions into my sex-dull relationship with Megan would end in an uncontrolled blast of white-hot semen before it'd even really started.

But Skylar – bright as a ten-watt bulb, but oh-so-blessed in the sex department – sensed my impending rupture and slowed the flow by sliding her hand up my shaft, pinching me tight just under the hood. I dug my fingernails into the wood of the ping-pong table and willed the boiling sperm in my balls back down to a simmer.

Skylar grinned up at me from her plump knees, white teeth clenching my swollen cap, fingers circle-squeezing my shaft until my balls turned blue again. "I thought you were gonna blow it there for a second, baby," she mouthed, not realizing the full extent of the truth she spoke.

I'd picked the green-eyed, bleached-blonde fleshpot up at a seedy downtown nightclub. The kind of place a respectable citizen like myself normally wouldn't be caught dead in; the kind of place that had me scared and second-guessing as soon as I'd pushed the padded leather door open.

But I loved Megan dearly – despite her unwillingness to try anything new – and I wasn't about to let our four-year relationship founder on the rocks of boredom without even attempting to jolt it back to life. So, I'd put on some false charm, and a padded wallet and pair of Jockeys, and picked the tipsy blonde up and brought her home. For demonstration purposes only. And now she was glibly bouncing my cockhead around on the end of her tongue while Megan – hopefully – watched from outside the rec shed, behind the small, blackened window that was actually tinted on the inside, rather than the outside.

Skylar pulled my cock aside and asked, "Ever had a girl go all the way down on you, baby?" Her eyes sparkled with pride.

"N-no," I choked. "But g-go right ahead."

That's what it was all about, after all – shocking Megan into the realization that sex could and should be more than just missionary in and out and off. She was a shy, quiet, 'still waters run deep' kind of woman, with a Puritanical streak of sexual sobriety that ran a Catholic mile wide. She was the type who liked to be shown rather than told what to do, and since she considered how-to sex tapes 'filth', I was showing her in the most vivid, realistic, and radical of ways.

Skylar grabbed onto my tightened sack and squeezed,

111

squirmed my balls around with her fingers. I arched with delight. Then she recaptured my bobbing cap in her wet-hot mouth and began her breathtaking descent.

"Jesus!" I croaked, watching her thick lips inch down, down my pulsating erection.

I'd thought about just hiring a prostitute, but concluded that would only cheapen the thing. Plus, I wanted to show Megan – along with the different techniques for above-and-beyond sexual satisfaction – that I was still desirable, that if she wouldn't love me in multiple ways, others would. Skylar dressed like a hooker, but her enthusiasm, sloppiness, and overall pudginess gave her away as an amateur.

The goodtime girl went cross-eyed watching her own mouth engulf my pole. Then she choked two-thirds of the way down, yanking me, awash in saliva, out of her gasping mouth. She looked up and giggled apologetically, then sucked air into her overgrown lungs and took right up where she'd left off, devouring my prick in a headlong rush for the short n' curly roots of all men's evil. Megan would barely touch my 'penis', let alone put her mouth anywhere near it.

Snot bubbled out of Skylar's flared nostrils, her breath puffing hot and humid on to my groin, her mouth and then throat bulging as she lip-crawled the last few exhilarating centimetres down my cock, into my fur. "Sweet Jesus, yes!" I groaned in admiration and jubilation.

I shook so badly the ping-pong table started jumping up and down. The plywood walls of the brightly-lit shed seemed to close in on me, the stuffy temperature soaring. I gasped for air, staring into Skylar's teary eyes. Her red face was right up against my skin, mouth and nose in my pubes, six inches of Tim Hudson buried and pulsing inside the girl. I felt her tongue snake out and lick at my balls, and I jerked with joy.

I prayed that Megan was taking shorthand notes out there in the darkness, because the sexual pressure was beyond anything I'd ever experienced before, and it was building and building and building. My blood boiled along with my balls, the wet and warmth and vice-like tightness incredible.

"Fuck!" I bayed at the bare light bulb dangling from the ceiling, not giving a tinker's damn that Megan considered profanity 'coarse'.

Tears of mascara streamed down Skylar's chubby cheeks, her watery eyes shining, her gleeful tongue caressing my balls. Her mouth and throat constricted around my surging cock, and I feared total meltdown. But then she suddenly snapped her head back, dropping me out of her mouth in a gush of hot spit. Leaving me dripping, dangling on the very slippery edge of ecstasy.

"Wanna fuck now, baby?" she inquired, grasping my slickened pole and tugging.

"Yes," I gulped. "Tit-fuck." I had to squeeze in as much variety as I could − for the edification of my girlfriend − before I blew my cool.

Skylar eagerly cooperated, grabbing up her hanging jugs and exposing her breastbone to my twitching cock, rolling her fat, rosy nipples. I pulled my fingers out of the ping-pong table and got a grip on myself, steering my enraged cock into the girl's cleavage, sliding snugly up and in between her hefty tits. She quickly closed the tan-lined flesh over my dick, sealing me in heat and wetness and softness all over again.

"Fuck my tits, baby!" she urged, happily juggling the mass of her boobs around.

I covered her hands on her breasts with my own

sweaty hands and pumped my hips, pushing my ramrod cock back and forth in her suffocating cleavage. It felt blissfully wicked, riding a woman's chest like that, fucking her tits, the superheated sex tunnel turning my pistoning pipe molten. Megan's breasts were nowhere near as large as Skylar's, but they could cradle a cock – if she let them.

Skylar and I stared down at my pumped-up hood peek-a-booing in and out of the top of her velvety cleavage, the voluptuous blonde's chin going triple and her tongue stretching out to meet my thrusting. I churned my hips like a madman, squeezing the girl's hands and her jiggling tits, torquing up the pressure to the blow-off point.

Until *I* pulled back, just short of eruption. There were more positions to explore, to demonstrate, and time and endurance were running short.

I pushed Skylar down on to her hands, as well as knees, and then dropped in behind her – doggy-style; a position Megan was never bitch enough to try. Then I grabbed onto the girl's chunky cheeks and kneaded the smooth, heavy butt-flesh, before probing her with my cock again, seeking the third sex opening of the evening.

I found her wetness, and hit it with my hardness, gliding deep inside her dripping pussy in one sweet, smooth motion. We both moaned. I grasped her waist and moved my hips, spanking her tanlined ass with my body, pumping her cunt with my cock.

"Yeah, do me, baby!" she shrieked encouragement, bum and body shuddering.

Sweat rolled off the twisted expression on my face and splashed down onto the two-eyes tattoo that looked up at me from Skylar's lower back, as I gritted my teeth and flung myself at the girl, pounding raging cock into silken pussy. The wet smack of flesh against flesh filled the stifling shack, the spicy smell of sex hanging heavy in the breathless air. I shot a squint-eyed glance over at the blackened window, picturing straight-laced little Megan on the other side, violet eyes wide and kewpie doll mouth hanging open. I was doing this for her, for us – couldn't she see that?

"I'm comin', baby!" Skylar bleated, reading my ragged mind. She furiously rubbed her clit, brazen body rocking in rhythm to my frantic thrusting.

"No-no! Not yet!" I yelped, slamming on the sexual brakes. "There's one more position I have to show her – do … for you."

I pulled my brimming cock out of the blonde's sodden sex and made myself even wetter with some spit. Then I spat manmade lube onto Skylar's bum, and she smeared it between her cheeks, knowing where I was cock-headed. I shoved my hood past her fingers and poked her final sexhole.

"Butt-fuck me, baby!" the ever-accommodating girl squealed, shoving back, swallowing me up with her ass.

I plugged her gripping chute just as deep as I'd penetrated her mouth and cleavage and pussy. Then I pried her cheeks apart to make sure Megan knew exactly where I was – buried in another woman's bum. Yes, it was possible, my dear. I regripped Skylar's waist and started fucking her ass.

"Yeah, baby! Yeah!" she cried, frantically buffing her clit as I stuffed her chute.

This was the tightest and hottest sex orifice yet, and I quivered from tip-to-toe with eroticism, body and cock on fire. I pounded and pounded the girl's rippling bum. Until the insanity and wanton sensuality overwhelmed and came crashing down upon me.

Skylar's body shook uncontrollably on the end of my dick, her butt cheeks dancing deliciously as she stroked herself – as I cock-stroked her, and me – to blistering orgasm. "Jesus Fucking Christ almighty, here I come!" I bellowed, head spinning and body exploding. I just barely had enough wherewithal and audacity to add, "In your mouth! In your mouth!"

I wrenched myself out of the blonde's ass and jumped to my feet, Skylar spinning around and scrambling under my blazing cock, sucking me into her mouth even as she still tremored with her own orgasm. I clutched at her hair and let loose, blasting my passion, topping off the erotic demonstration with sizzling fireworks.

The corners of Skylar's mouth leaked semen, as she earnestly swallowed over and over. I spasmed with every fiery spurt, the blonde and I showing my girlfriend a level of sexual communion and commitment I only hoped she'd take to heart, and bed.

It was three long, cold nights later before I finally received a response to my radical sexual intervention from Megan. She'd hardly spoken to me since I'd sent Skylar packing with a mouthful of my thanks, would barely look at me. I felt for sure that our long-term relationship had ended with a bang, and I kicked myself for not getting the blonde's phone number.

When I arrived home from work on that third night, and called out for Megan, there wasn't any answer. Just a folded note on the dining room table. I opened it up with trembling fingers, my body and psyche sagging as I faced the inevitable.

'See me at the rec shed,' was all the note said.

I stiff-legged it out into the night and in behind the shed, trying to get a bead on the situation by peeking in the tinted window. And I saw my naked girlfriend getting her pussy licked by a naked man.

"Yes!" I exulted, pumping my fist into the air, eating up the erotic sight.

Megan was wearing only a pair of shiny, black high-heel shoes I'd never seen before, leaning against the ping-pong table, the man on his knees in between her slim, spread legs, vigorously tonguing her pussy. Her eyes were closed and her shimmering, raven hair hung loose about her pale shoulders, her red-painted fingernails digging into the bald head of the man.

His muscled body was bronze in colour, tattooed all over. He was bobbing that shaven skull of his up and down as he lapped and lapped at my girlfriend's furry pussy, his wedge of a tongue gleaming pink like a sexual organ in the bright bulb-light, showing me exactly how to do something I'd never done before. As Megan was explicitly demonstrating that what was good for the gander, was good for the goose.

This gandering gander couldn't have been happier, though, because I knew now that our relationship was very much alive, our sex life set on fire. I took a quick glance around the back lane, didn't see any other Peeping Toms out there in the dark, so gave myself even more exposure, unzipping and pulling my erection out of my pants and stroking. The sight of another man sexing up my Megan in a position I'd never dared dream of turned me on big-time, and I urged the lusty pair on with every excited flick of my wrist.

The man of bronze and tats thoroughly tongue-lashed Megan's twat, before finally pulling his face back and licking his sticky lips. He turned his head to the side to spit out a stray pube and that's when I recognized the dude with the soul patch. It was Chavez from the loading

117

docks at work!

My hand froze on my pole, and I swallowed so hard I almost had my Adam's apple for dinner. But Megan smiled contentedly at the blackened window, winking at me. Then she pulled her pussy lips apart and got Chavez to spear her pink with his sticker, fuck her with his cock-hard tongue.

"Slut!" I hissed exuberantly, cranking up my dong again.

The big man crushed Megan's creamy-white buttocks in his ham-hands and savagely pumped his tongue into her exposed sex. Her little body shook with pleasure, her small breasts jumping every time Chavez drove his tongue home. And when the guy at last retracted his oral pleasure tool, latched his thick lips on to her puffed-up clit and started sucking, she full-body shuddered with the erotic impact. Demonstrating a level of sexual arousal and perversity I'd never seen from her before.

When she got sucked too close to the edge, she quickly pushed Chavez back from her pussy and said something to the guy. He obediently scooped up and cradled her right foot in his hands, began kissing and licking her porcelain arch where it was enshrined in the slut-shoe.

Megan was getting the stud to give me further demonstration of what I could do to spice up her sex life, and mine. He yanked off her high heels, fully exposing her delicate peds. Then he slashed his tongue across her red-painted toes, squirmed it in between the wriggling piggies, one at a delectable time. He captured my girlfriend's big toe in his mouth and sucked on it, pulled on the other with his lips. Before taking the exquisitely tapered tips of her peds into his huge maw and sucking on both of her feet at once. Megan shivered, her crimson

118

lips forming an 'O'!

I leered and learned, urgently fisting my iron dong, shaking with excitement like Megan, the both of us stoked on wicked, untapped carnality. She got the giant to let go of her feet and stand up on his, his vein-striated cock bobbing up dangerously long and hard. Megan took the giant organ in her tiny hand and squeezed, and Chavez grabbed onto her breasts, stuffed them into his mouth.

He mauled my girlfriend's soft, ivory breast-flesh, slapping at her puffy, pink nipples with his tongue, as she clung to his thundercock like a little lady clings to the end of a big dog's leash. Chavez chewed on her nipples, swallowing up almost all of one tit and pulling hungrily on it and then doing the same to the other. She had him thoroughly work over her breasts, not the cursory rub and tug I normally gave them. I stroked faster and faster, my breath steaming up the window.

Finally, Megan pushed her lover (my fellow employee) down onto his back on the indoor-outdoor carpeting – onto the very same spot where I'd fucked Skylar like I'd never fucked anyone before, three nights earlier. Then she climbed aboard the rugged man, straddling his angry head, easing her pussy down over his open mouth. She screamed as he bit his dirty fingernails into her buttocks and tore into her cunt with his tongue.

She glanced towards the window, at me, her eyes glazed over with lust. Then she picked Chavez's fuckclub up off his ribbed stomach and without hesitation took the enormous crown into her mouth. It was the sweet sixty-nine she'd never been willing to share with me before.

Chavez fervently tongued Megan's snatch, as she lowered her head and captured more and more of his meat in the heated confines of her mouth, started sucking

119

on the pillar of cock. I spat down onto my prick, greasing it like I knew Megan's pussy was greased, like Chavez's cock was being oiled with my girlfriend's hot saliva.

Megan tucked her shiny locks in behind her right ear as she energetically bobbed her head up and down on Chavez's dong, so I could fully see and appreciate the oral sex she was performing. I saw it, all right, and greatly appreciated it, fisting furiously as she sucked hard and long on the guy, as he devoured her pussy, plugged a cunt-slick finger into her butthole and pumped.

I could hear their animal moaning and groaning right through the plywood, could almost taste my woman's hot, tangy juices. The sights and sounds and strange feelings I felt at watching my girlfriend go wild with another man soon sent me boiling over the edge.

We came as a threesome; me buckling, blasting the wall of the shed with my ecstasy; Megan trembling out-of-control with clit-stimulated orgasms, tugging superheated spray out of Chavez's bucking cock and into her open mouth. And damned if my girl didn't make the big guy hold and cuddle her after it was all over, giving me one final lesson for the night – and the nights to come.

# Bestseller
## by Judith Roycroft

"She's insatiable, mate. You wouldn't believe it!" Clutching his Fosters, Mike lifted it to his parched lips and took a long swig. "Aah. Needed that." He crumpled the can in his hand, then set it back on the bar. He turned to his long time mate and added, "Thirsty work, all that lovin'." He grinned.

Momentarily speechless, Cameron stared. "And you're complaining? Come off it, Mike! A man'd have to be nuts to grouse about too much nookie! You're living every guy's fantasy."

"Not bellyaching. Just tellin' you."

"So, what's Jen working on now? Another Jackie Collins' blockbuster?" Cameron sniggered.

"So she says. There's no other reason I'm thrown on the floor and set upon every time I step inside that door." Mike recalled the last four weeks with a satisfied grin. Ever since Jen had progressed from penning short stories to writing her first novel, she had been plagued with difficulties over the sex scenes. At times writing anatomical impossibilities. And since having this pointed out to her – by Mike himself – she insisted on acting out all scenes.

The first night he arrived in from work to find her

leaning nonchalantly against the dining room table wearing only a lacy red suspender belt and black stockings, it had been all go. Mike had needed no further encouragement and when Jen presented her pert little rear to him while sauntering across to the sofa, he thought he would explode before he had a chance to touch her. And now, with a knowing wink at his old buddy, he gripped his crotch and drawled, "Gotta go, Cameron. Little lady's awaitin'."

And he ambled off with his mate's envious comments resounding in his ears.

Jen was tapping the toe of her shiny black boot. She nibbled on her lip. Where was that man? Didn't he like all this attention? Most men would die for what she was dishing out to Mike every night, and besides, she had just finished composing a really steamy scene, her fingers flying over the keyboard, even as the lower half of her body shifted and squirmed. Earlier, unable to bear the discomfort any longer, the scene coming to life as she visualized the hero's long tanned fingers stroking the woman's soft thighs, the wonderfully sinewy chest crushing the small but perfectly rounded breasts, the moist male lips seeking her heroine's – Jen had thrown back her chair and sprinted down the hall.

And failed to find Mike propped up in front of the TV as she had expected. She fumed for several minutes, and somehow managed to force herself back to the computer to complete her writing amid further wriggles and writhing, but if Mike didn't appear soon, she'd burst with the need for relief.

Satisfying herself wasn't a problem of course. Despite regular great sex with her husband, she often locked herself in the bathroom with one of his girly magazines, and brought her body to a swift climax. Not that she ever contemplated being with a woman. What she managed with the magazines clasped in her hand was to visualise a thick shaft plunging into one of those welcoming wet pussies, and it excited her.

Just thinking about all this shot tingles through her. She took a sip of Chardonnay. *To hell with it, I will go and have a finger fuck!*

A car door slammed and Jen dashed to the window, slopping wine on to her hand. She sucked the sweet spill of liquid dribbling down her wrist.

"About time," she muttered, setting her glass down on the sill. Didn't the man know she was on fire?

Mike didn't want to appear too eager. Never hurt to keep them guessing was his motto, but even so, the door flung back out of his grasp and bounced off the doorstop. Apparently he wasn't the only one eager for a good old fuck.

Acutely aware of the rapid swelling of his dick, tight jeans hugging his throbbing bulge, Mike's excitement soared.

Jen's get-up was better than the last time, he noted. Very imaginative, as with a slow smile he swept his gaze over his curvy little wife. She was wearing black jackboots, those alone sufficient to stir a man to the heights of ecstasy. A silver thong that covered not a thing, and small red circles balanced on her nipples. And a bright red smile.

"Je-sus!" If only she had started her erotic writings years ago during all those relatively lean years. Those times their lovemaking had become routine, and he'd been every bit as bored as Jen appeared to be, but now – *now,* she had a ferocious appetite. And he had that babe

123

Jackie Collins to thank.

"Where's the whip?" Mike joked, dying to jump out of his jeans and get on with it.

For a moment, Jen's smile slipped. "I don't resort to such crude props in my scenes, Mike," she rebuked him.

*Oh, yeah? What do you call those boots?* But he wasn't about to argue. Far more important things on his mind.

Before he had time to remove his shirt, Jen was bearing down on him. Her feathery touch slid along his arms and he shivered. Being a shorty, she got on tippy-toes to place her luscious wet mouth on his. As her tongue slipped decisively between his lips, he nearly came in his pants. *Crikey! None of that, mate.* He wanted to bury himself inside his wife's lovely snatch before he let loose. Having to wait was getting a helluva lot more difficult as her tongue slid in and out of his mouth. He inhaled a spicy mix of cinnamon and fresh nutmeg, her legacy from tonight's dinner, he assumed, as Jen drew away.

With a smirk she popped the remaining shirt buttons, placed a fingertip on the rapid pulse at his throat. Tossed him a smile like the temptress she was. Then she bent her head and licked away the film of sweat that was already coating his skin. He tensed; trembled again when she placed her hot little palms over the nipples hiding in his chest hair. When she pressed her thumbs against the pebble-hard disks, he jerked back, sucking in his breath, and prayed that she would hurry up and get to the main course.

His wife stilled, adopted a look of fierce concentration, which was disconcertingly clinical. Mike growled and grabbed her hand, guiding it lower down his body.

"Mike! You're breaking my concentration. I'm trying to write a book here."

"I call it torturing your husband." As he caught the smile that twitched and radiated from her eyes, he blustered, "Hey – nothing too weird, mind!"

"Would I do that to you, sweetie?" Jen purred. "But it's given me the most marvellous idea. All we need do is play it out. See if it works."

Sinking onto the carpet, Jen dragged her man along with her. Her tongue zinged with the taste of ale from Mike's mouth. As Mike stretched out alongside her, she took hold of his zip, sliding it open, then tugged at his jeans. Slowly, seductively, down, purring like a contented kitten.

"My, what a big boy you are," Jen said huskily, as she released his erection from his briefs. She snatched a cheeky kiss on the tip of his cock, then jumped to her feet. "Be back in a minute."

"Hey! Where're you going? Come back here, you little minx!" Mike sat up, his dick throbbing painfully. He watched her pert little bum swaying. He wanted to bend her over, take her from behind. "Jen!"

"Patience, my love," Jen called from the kitchen.

Mike heard the fridge door open. She wasn't getting something to eat, was she? Mike groaned, collapsed back onto the floor. What a time to skip out and open the bloody fridge!

When he heard the clinking that heralded his wife's return, he looked up. What the hell was in that bowl?

As if he had spoken aloud, Jen grinned, tipping the bowl so he could take a look for himself.

"Ice? Oh no you don't. You're not sticking that stuff on me."

"Oh, don't be such a party-pooper. You'll love it, I

promise. Here, just try this one cube then, you little yellow-belly."

As the sparkling cube touched his cock, Mike bit down on his lip to keep from yelping.

"Feel good?" Jen slid the ice up and down the length of his rod, round and round, the base, the head, even his balls.

"Jes-us! It's bloody cold!" Mike shuddered.

"Well, it is a block of ice, you daft thing."

And as she rubbed and he felt the ice melting with his body heat, his cock began to feel damn great! Stiff, rock-hard. Skin about to burst. *Wow! This is something else!*

The heat suddenly encasing him was so intense after the chill that his backside reared up off the floor in shock. Only Jen's hands pinning him down stopped his cock from ramming right down her throat. He lay back, basked in pleasure. Let her warm mouth soothe the tight skin. Hot tongue lapped at moisture left by the ice. Mike tried to choke out a question as to where she'd learnt this new trick but pleasure overtook any curiosity and really, he couldn't have cared less. Just so long as she continued lapping at him like a little pug dog, bringing him to the brink of climax.

When her mouth left him, he opened one eye. "Don't … don't stop now, babe." Jen grinned mischievously. Seconds later, he discovered why.

Two handfuls of ice encased his cock in a glacial sheath. The bite to his skin was so erotically intense that Mike tried to wriggle away, involuntarily spurring his orgasm on. Christ! He couldn't hold back.

He erupted like a modern day Krakatoa.

"Right on!" cried Jen, punching a fist in the air.

As Mike continued to gush as impressively as a Tivoli

fountain, Jen sat back on her heels, staring in awe. It was almost impossible to believe a body contained so much of the stuff. The scent of sex rose with each spurt; a potent lure, and she could hardly wait.

"My turn now," Jen chirped, once Mike's rod began to deflate.

Mike's breath slowed. "I'm all blown out, babe."

Jen pouted.

With his breathing on an even keel, Mike defended himself. "I would if I could but I can't. You know I'm all for equal orgasms. But, crikey, baby. What are you trying to do? Kill a man?"

Refusing to take him seriously, Jen walked smartly away from him. Then with a swift glance over her shoulder, she threw a coy smile. Next, she bent over, placed her palms on the floor, giving her man a stellar view of plump lips shielding her slit. She wriggled her bum. *If that doesn't give you a thrill, I'll eat my hat!*

Hearing the sharp intake of air, Jen knew she had him and, smirking, sauntered back over to join Mike. No way was she missing out tonight. Her little treasure box was on fire and she needed Mike's hose to snuff it out. Long after he practised fire drill, of course. She'd let him know when she was ready to be doused.

So often Jen wanted Mike passive, to act out scenes. This last one was an unmitigated success. And now she deserved some loving.

Straddling his waist, she shifted her thong aside, allowed her pussy to touch his skin, and was rewarded with another sharp intake of breath.

"I'll have you ready to go in no time."

Wriggling around on top of him, she felt the once forlorn penis begin to rise. Slowly. But it was getting there. She shimmied higher, until she straddled his jaw.

127

Knowing what was expected, Mike stuck out his tongue and began to lap along the wetness of her slit. She felt the sting of his teeth, the soothing softness of tongue that followed. With a loud groan Jen positioned herself so more pressure was on her clit. His tongue flicked, gently at first, then hard and fast. Bathed in a warm glow, nearly there at the pinnacle, one part of her wanted instant release, another part wanted it to drift on and on for ever.

In the end her arousal was too explosive to contain; waves of ecstasy feathered, gathered as swiftly as storm clouds, and she embraced tingles that shivered through her, overpowering all reason.

As she sat back on Mike's belly, his hand rode frantically over her hip to the top of the leather boot. Slipped between her thighs. His fingers stroked the moist pleats of her sex as she purred with pleasure, then focused skilfully on the hard pleasure bud at her centre.

"Oh! Oh yes! Harder! Please don't … don't stop."

"Crikey, babe. Where do you get these little get-ups you wear?" Mike panted, as he worked her clit. Somehow they were far more sexy than having her completely naked.

As Mike peeled away the tiny red sticker with his free hand, the residue of gum pulled at her nipple, stretching it, inciting her further.

"My hero would then lap the slight stickiness from my heroine's rose-petal –" She gasped. "Mike! What are you doing? You're veering from my script!"

Ignoring her, Mike sucked one nipple into his mouth, while his thumb dislodged the red dot from the other. She groaned, her hands coming up to his hair, pulling, tugging, frantic in their quest, her arousal escalating by the second. He smelled of beer and salt, a slight smokiness, as his leg pressed between hers and she began to ride him. The pressure was exactly right to stimulate her tiny shaft as she ground herself against his knee.

Then the bugger laughed.

"Hey, Jen. Remember when you had your characters engage in their first romp? That description you wrote of the chick standing on one leg while she wrapped the other around the guy's neck? Some feat!" He buckled with laughter, tumbling her sideways as she belted him across the head.

She remembered. Hadn't taken that earlier criticism too well either, and had flounced off to her study. That's when he called out after her, suggesting they could play out her positions. Just to ensure they were possible and perhaps improve the scene. And when he sneaked up behind her, he'd lifted her by the waist, demanded she part her legs, and rammed his cock home. God! Was that a turn-on, or what? She'd come almost immediately. Both so highly aroused, they climaxed within seconds of one another. After that, they often rehearsed a scene.

With the memory of that wonderful fuck spurring her on, Jen straddled him, rubbing her damp sex against his, effectively cutting off his amusement. Her breasts skimmed his chest as she lifted herself for one second, then plunged down on to his waiting shaft. When he filled her, she began to move, slowly, up and down. Long, delicious strokes of contentment, aware only of the sensations shimmying through her. She felt Mike flex inside her and as he lifted his hips to link completely with her again, she began to ride him once more, thumping down on him, feeling the spread of her swollen labia at the base of his cock.

Suddenly, Mike's fingers dug into her hips, and he hoisted her up, only to plunge her down, spreading her distended love lips with his rod, again and again, until the scent of sex misted in the air and their combined breath laboured.

"Come with me," Jen said, stopping suddenly.

Mike groaned. He didn't want to stop and tried to tell her, with powerful thrusts into that lovely opening that was so hot and wet, he never wanted to leave it. "I'll play your clit," he panted, the pad of his thumb homing in. "Then you won't want to disappear."

When Jen clamoured off of him, he cursed loudly.

"What now? You sure know how to pick your moments," he grizzled.

Her reply was to take his hand. "Get up," she ordered, and Mike found himself doing so, then allowing her to drag him through the room and out the back door.

"Hey, you're not thinking of doing it out here." Mike glanced up at the yellow glow of the neighbour's front room. He covered his jewels with one hand.

"Yes I am, scaredy-cat." Catching Mike's line of vision, she laughed. "Thought we'd give old Jack a thrill."

"More like give him a blasted heart attack. You willing to risk that?'

It appeared she was, because she flopped down on the lawn and with a small squeal as her bum met damp grass, she settled back, spread thighs beckoning him.

One quick glance at the old guy's curtainless window, and Mike thought what the hell. Maybe Jen was right. Maybe this would make Jack's day. Or night, rather.

When Mike lay atop her, she lifted her legs for deeper penetration. And sighed. Once impaled, she rested for a moment, the stem of his magic stick flush with her opening. His pubic bone pressed hers, stimulating her clitoris. With a few delicious squirms, Jen enjoyed the fullness of engorged cock inside her. She loved the stop-start of loving. Reaching the very height of ecstasy, then plummeting to earth again. It meant her orgasm was ten times as intense. Evening fragrances curled seductively in the air. Crickets sang lustily. Jen giggled. Maybe they were shagging, too!

She loved the way Mike nuzzled the sensitive skin below her ear, taking tiny nips as she murmured happily. The night scented magnolia stirred in a soft breeze, whispered across her skin. What could be better than making love in the moonlight with the man of her dreams? A huge sigh of contentment and she was off again. Lifting her body, she synchronised thrusts with her adorable man.

Jen's satiny sheath gripped him. Mike grunted every time he pounded into her, just as she liked him to do. His breath stirred wisps of her hair. He was bursting with love for this delectable creature who excited him more than anyone he could imagine. Something caused him to glance up. A white face peered down on the shadowy figures rutting in a sliver of moonlight. Jen was right! This was bloody exhilarating! He pounded into her. Again and again, bent on giving a top performance, just as his little lady liked it.

Suddenly, Mike rolled with his partner, until it was Jen's perky bum on display for the guy next door. A pity old Jack wouldn't be able to make out the puffy folds of her sex lips in this light. That was a sight to set the pulse skyrocketing.

On that thought, Mike felt himself begin to blow. Jen's sex clamped his.

Cries of mutual passion rose in a crescendo around them as they both gave into spasms of pleasure rocking their bodies.

\*　　　\*　　　\*

Several weeks later Mike staggered into the *Old Cock and Young Bull*. Old cock is right, he grimaced. Week after week of mind-blowing sex had left Mike all shagged out, as he hobbled towards the bar to catch up with his best buddy.

Cameron greeted him salaciously. "Too much of a good thing, mate? It's the woman who's supposed to end up bow-legged."

"I want it and yet I don't," Mike confided to Cameron while waiting for his pint to be pulled.

"You sound like a woman now. Can't make up your mind."

Mike downed his beer, followed with a satisfied sigh. "Good news is, I've had a reprieve. I'm out of town next week on the Smithson job. Best of all, Jen's finished the book. Look forward to some early nights, I can tell you. And I'm talking about snooze-land."

Cameron laughed. "Not many guys would moan about being jumped on every night. With my better half, I've resorted to begging. She may as well lock it away in a safety deposit box a hundred miles away. Just as damn difficult to get at."

Right now Mike envied Cameron. "Wrenched my back a week ago. In the middle of a great shag it was. Reckon the old bloke next door has a new lease of life. One good thing to come out of it, I suppose." Mike went on to tell how several romps ended up out on the lawn. Right under Jack's nose. "Thank God the book's winging its way out of the house."

"Clever old Jen!" Cameron said, envious of the conjured vision of sex beneath the stars with a willing partner. One blessed with a voracious appetite, to boot. "Didn't think Jen'd stick at writing. So, the book's off at the publishers. She gonna wait to hear? Or is she starting another?" Cameron slurped the head off his third beer of the night.

"Yeah. Dead keen now, but at least I'll get a breather. Reckon she's done enough research to last her through several manuscripts." A sliver of uncertainty struck Mike. "Knowing Jen though …"

"What's it to be this time?"

"She's writing about a woman who seduces her husband's best friend."

Cameron spluttered into his beer, firing foamy droplets across the polished teak bar.

# Shower Block
## by Eva Hore

My boyfriend Brad and I were camping down at the beach. After a day of surfing and partying I was tired, sweaty and stinking of smoke from the campfires. I decided to have a shower before hitting the sack.

Entering the block I heard water running and the giggling sounds of a man and woman coming from one of the cubicles where steam from the hot running water lingered. Intrigued, I entered the stall next to them and instantly their voices subsided to whispers. Wanting them to think I was unaware of them being in there together, I turned on the taps and began humming.

Then I quietly climbed up on the bench and peeked over the top. They were both naked. Water cascaded down their tanned bodies as they soaped each other up. She was pulling at his cock, her foam-covered hand slipping up and down the slippery shaft. I watched in awe as he grabbed at her huge breasts, which looked like melons, and gave them a good washing, taking care to tweak her nipples before his mouth descended upon them and his other hand disappeared between her thighs.

My pussy twitched madly as his tongue flickered over her nipples before he sucked one deep into his mouth, stretching it out as she squealed with delight. She grabbed hold of his head, smothering him into her breasts as water gushed over his hair and face before he broke free to take in some air. Checking to make sure there was no one else in the shower block, I quietly removed my clothes and continued to watch.

Being naked, and in such close proximity, with only a wall to separate us made this an absolute turn-on. As I watched, my hand roamed around my pubic hair and I imagined him in here with me soaping me up, running his hands over my tits and then down further over my pussy and into my slit.

I was wishing Brad was in here with me and wondering why we never did anything so risqué. We always talked about our fantasies, what we'd do one day, but never acted upon them.

Holding my breath, I watched as he stood behind her and bent her forward. His massive cock, all shiny and wet, probed around her arse cheeks before it slipped into her pussy. She placed her hands against the wall and pushed back, grinding her arse into him, while his fingers gripped her hips and he slammed his rock-hard cock into her. The slapping of their wet bodies and her moaning seemed to echo in the quiet room.

I was rubbing my clit, enjoying being the voyeur, but when I reached a peak where I knew I was about to come, I sat down on the edge of the bench, placed my feet on the opposite wall and opened my legs wide. I pulled back the hood over my clit, my scent filling my nostrils while their moaning filled my ears.

I rubbed quickly, enjoying what I was doing and before long my body arched and spasmed as an orgasm shook through me. I had my lips pursed tight, trying hard not to moan as my juices dribbled down the crack of my arse. My chest heaved and my breasts shook and my legs quivered as I kept coming.

Not satisfied with just my fingers, I grabbed my shampoo bottle and inserted it inside me. Inching it in I began to fuck myself with it, imagining the guy in the cubicle was in here with me and it was his cock fucking me instead.

About to come again, I rammed the bottle deeper, crushing my breast, rolling my fingers over my nipple, pinching the flesh. My head fell back on the verge of a mighty orgasm and I looked up through half-closed eyes to see that the couple now were watching *me*. Dropping the bottle I stood on shaky legs unsure of what I should do as I tried to find my towel and cover up.

'Hey!' I said outraged, 'what … what do you think you're doing?'

'Want to join us?' the guy asked, his handsome face beaming down at me.

'I … er … I …' I stammered, unable to speak properly, the very thought of them having just watched me turning me into a blithering idiot.

'Come on, we won't tell anyone,' she giggled. 'We know you were watching us before.'

I didn't hesitate then. Leaving my clothes, I ran out naked and into their cubicle. I've never done anything so bold and uncertain before and was unsure of how to go about it. I didn't want to come across naive and stupid, even though I was. I needn't have worried though. They sandwiched me between them and the two of them soaped me up, running their hands deliciously all over my body. The guy pulled my head back to kiss me and the woman sucked my nipples into her mouth.

I've never felt so sexy in my life. She crushed my breasts, her fingers digging in deep before sucking harder, drawing on the nipple, sucking, sucking and then licking while his cock probed my arse. I orgasmed immediately, my knees buckling while I gasped for breath, unable to believe anything could be this mind-blowing.

It was fucking amazing and when she worked her mouth lower to nibble on my clit before sticking her fingers inside my already saturated cunt I actually swooned. I was so overcome with lust that I could barely stand.

The guy's finger was poking at my puckered hole and he soaped up his hand while he caressed my cheeks, his fingers slipping down the crack and then slowly inching in as he gently bent me over. She rose, grabbing at one of my breasts and with her fingers still in my cunt and his finger in my hole it took only seconds for me to come.

As my juices ran down her fingers she murmured to her boyfriend.

'She's hot for you, man,' and as quick as a flash he bent me further forward and rammed that fantastic cock of his straight into my saturated pussy. I was tottering on the tips of my toes as the water was cascading down between our bodies. The woman massaged my tits, pulling at my nipples, squeezing hard until I nearly screamed out while he fucked me ferociously.

Then with my body weak and tingling all over the guy laid me on the small ledge, one foot flat on the floor while the other was pressed hard against the wall. He threw his fat cock into my open mouth and I gobbled it up greedily.

He smacked my gaping pussy, electrifying the lips as I sucked him off. She pushed his hand away and went down on me smothering my pussy with her hot mouth. I sucked frantically, desperately wanting to please these people and enjoying every second.

Then we changed positions. The woman climbed up on the seat too, lifting one leg over her man's shoulder while he fingered her cunt. I couldn't stop looking at her perky lips stretched wide as four of his fingers fucked her.

I'd been fingering myself while I watched and now eager to taste my first pussy, I sidled up to her and began licking out her snatch. With her leg still resting over his shoulder, I licked from her hole all the way up and around her lips, pulling his fingers away so I could spend time tantalizing her clit. He too then lowered his head and as our tongues lashed against each other we brought her to an orgasmic peak, her juices oozing over both our mouths and chins.

They were insatiable and now he sat on the bench and motioned for me to straddle his cock. I jumped on quickly, eager to become impaled upon him. With my feet resting on the seat he held me by my arse cheeks and bounced me up and down while his girlfriend slipped her finger in and out of my hole.

'Oh God, yeah,' I moaned as my slippery cunt slid over his pulsating shaft.

I began to moan louder, not caring if anyone could hear, and thrashed my head from side to side while the guy nibbled hard on my nipples. Unable to stop myself, I cried out as my juices gushed from me, all over his lap and down his thighs. I held his head tightly against my breasts, breathless as I came again, and still he bounced me up and down until I thought I'd be split in two.

Finally he stopped and I collapsed against him, feeling his throbbing cock deep inside me while he now sucked my nipples delicately, swirling his tongue around before lapping at them, his breath causing goose bumps to break out all over my body.

'My turn,' the girl purred in my ear and as though in a daze I disentangled myself from him.

On shaky legs I stood, turned and kissed the girl full on the mouth while my hands grabbed at her enormous breasts. He pulled me back towards him and I felt his cock probe my hole, pulling my cheeks apart as he slowly inched his huge knob in. While he bent me further forward, she sat and my face practically fell into her lap. She lay back as much as she could, lifted her legs and flopped them over my shoulders and I dove down into her hairless snatch.

My knees did buckle and I swayed as he prised my cheeks further apart and then suddenly he was all the way in. Fucking my arse like that, was something I'd never experienced before and I loved it. I had no idea how he'd managed to manoeuvre himself in but I went wild, smothering my face in the woman's cunt, while he slammed in and out of me.

'Mary, you in here?' a voice cried out.

Shit it was my boyfriend Brad.

'Mary?' he asked again when I didn't answer.

'I'll … er … I'll be out in a minute,' I mumbled, trying to disengage myself from the two of them.

'Invite him in,' the guy leaned over me and whispered in my ear while still fucking my arse.

'What?' I gasped, my face wet with her juices.

'Invite him in,' his girlfriend giggled as she manoeuvred over to the door.

'Want to join me?' I asked, my voice quivering as I hoped I was making the right decision.

'Sure,' he laughed but the laughter died on his lips as the door opened and he saw me being fucked like some whore.

'What the …' he began.

The woman grabbed him and dragged him in.

'Fucking hell,' he said, stripping out of his clothes as we all squeezed in together.

The woman and I both ravished him, fighting over who was going to suck his cock first. Brad then picked me up and I jumped up to straddle his waist. His cock found my pussy immediately and I slid down his amazing shaft. The other guy sandwiched me in and then his cock was fucking my hole again.

With the two of them fucking me like that I came like a madwoman, screaming and crying. We spent hours in there, doing everything you can imagine to each other and more. It's the best fun I've had in the shower, and thank God there were no water restrictions on to dampen our lovemaking.

# Road Rage
## by Elizabeth Cage

Blazing heat and city traffic. Well, traffic jams, to be more precise. Not forgetting the stink of petrol fumes. A combination that always set Sam's stress levels shooting up, despite having spent the morning teaching a yoga class at the local fitness centre. All she wanted was to get home, put her feet up and slowly sip a long, cool, drink. With ice.

'What do you think the bloody indicator's for?' she yelled as yet another driver cut into her lane. Typical man. God, they were so rude. Put them behind the wheel of a car and they transformed into raging territorial Neanderthals. She glanced at her watch. Almost midday. This was going to take ages, unless she took decisive action. Luckily, Sam knew the area well. So, at the next turning, she shot off down a side road, intending to take a short cut. Despite weaving her way through a network of minor roads, she was making good time until she found herself in a narrow street with double-parked cars on both sides. Cautiously, she made her way down the centre, hoping she wouldn't meet any other traffic. Then she spotted a large white van driving towards her.

As she was nearly at the end of the street, Sam expected him to reverse into the one available parking space, allowing her to pass. But he didn't. He just kept coming.

'Move, you moron,' she cursed under her breath. If he didn't get out of her way soon, their vehicles would be almost touching. Why on earth didn't he reverse into the space and let her pass?

Seconds later, they were both forced to stop, their front bumpers practically touching.

'Would you please reverse?' she shouted through her open window.

'You reverse,' he retorted gruffly, his tattooed arm hanging over the door, his fingers drumming impatiently. She noticed that his head was shaved, and despite his clear blue eyes, he had a hard-boiled look about him.

'But there's nowhere for me to go,' she pointed out, trying to stay calm. Best to avoid confrontation in these situations.

He pointed behind her. Surely he wasn't expecting her to reverse all the way back along the street and onto the main road?

'I can't,' she replied. 'That would be dangerous.' Not to mention illegal. Anyway, why should she?

But to her amazement he just sat there, using his big van to try to intimidate her, the bully.

'I can't,' she repeated.

He stared straight ahead, just waiting for her to move. This was ridiculous. Neither of them could go anywhere. Surely he would have to see sense? As the minutes ticked by, anger welled up inside her. Sam hated reversing in narrow spaces, but if she didn't they would both be stuck. As he revved impatiently, she wondered if it was worth the hassle, trying to argue with a man like this. Sighing, she was about to put the car into reverse when he started hooting his horn. Then something snapped inside her.

Calmly, Sam turned the key and switched her engine off.

The van driver stared in disbelief as she picked up her newspaper and started to read. Ignoring his loud remonstrations, his shouting and swearing, Sam perused the Women's section before moving on to the theatre reviews.

'Move you silly tart,' he yelled.

'Screw you!' she replied, her tone even.

Narrowing his eyes, he edged his van so close that he was actually touching her bumper. Despite her apparently calm exterior, Sam was shaking inside but resolutely determined to stand her ground. Even so, her open-topped sports car wouldn't offer much protection if he decided to get nasty.

'Right,' he said. 'Two can play that game.' Everything went quiet as he switched his engine off.

Anxiously, Sam wondered what would happen next. It was a blisteringly hot day, with not a hint of a breeze to cool things down. She was sweating. There they were, two opponents, just facing each other out. Glaring, he got out of his van and sat on the bonnet in his black vest and shorts. Sam noticed that he was tanned, with a muscular torso. She could imagine him lifting weights, showing off in the gym. Under different circumstances she could have fancied him. Definitely would have, in fact. But after the way he'd behaved, she wouldn't give him the satisfaction of a friendly word, let alone anything more than that.

'You can't keep this up all day,' he shouted.

'Wanna bet?' she retorted furiously, more determined than ever. No way was she going to give in to this arrogant bastard.

As she sat in her car, Sam became aware that her halter neck top was digging into her skin. What she wouldn't give to be diving into a swimming pool at this

143

moment. Wiping sweat from her furrowed brow, she twisted her long blonde hair into a knot and fastened it behind her head with a scrunchie.

They glared at each other, the sun beating down. She felt like she was in a western film. As the time ticked by, she was reminded of High Noon. Eventually, though, after ten minutes of this he began to relent. Realising his aggressive tactics hadn't achieved the desired effect, he adopted a more conciliatory tone.

'Be reasonable, love,' he pleaded. 'My boss will kill me if I'm late with this delivery.'

'You should have thought of that,' Sam retorted.

He sighed. 'This is getting boring.' He stood up, wondering what to do next. She sensed he was now more anxious than she was. She was gaining the upper hand.

'What do I have to do to persuade you?' he asked.

'Say please.'

'Please,' he muttered ungraciously.

'That didn't sound very genuine.'

'Please,' he repeated.

'Pretty please. With bells on.'

He glared. 'Don't push your luck, girlie.'

She glared back. 'You move. I got here first.'

They were back to stalemate.

'Looks like we're stuck, then.'

'Sure does.'

Finally he growled, swore at her and got back into his van. Slamming the door shut, he turned the key.

'Yes, I've won,' Sam crowed to herself.

But there was no welcome throaty roar from his engine. He turned the key again. Nothing.

'It won't start.'

'You're having me on,' she said. 'You're just saying that so I have to move my car.'

144

'Don't be so childish.' He looked genuinely annoyed. 'The bloody van's dead as a doorknob.'

'This is ridiculous.' She couldn't let victory slip from her grasp, not when it was so close. 'Let me see.'

Sam got out of her car, peered into the van. He turned the key again. There was nothing, not even the sound of the starter motor turning.

'Does it have petrol?' she asked.

'Of course it does, you silly tart. I'm not a woman.'

'Hang on, mate. Before you go into a sexist rant, I'm neither silly nor a tart.'

'Well, unless you're a mechanic, which I somehow doubt –'

'I thought men were supposed to be the experts when it comes to all things vehicular.'

'What're you going on about?'

'If you can't fix it, then call the AA or something.'

'I'm not in the AA.'

'The RAC then.'

He shook his head.

'Typical man!' she exclaimed.

'You really are pissing me off now,' he said. 'I've got a good mind to put you over my knee and –'

'Give me a good spanking?' Sam laughed derisively. 'I'd like to see you try it.'

Their eyes locked, like two warriors about to do battle.

'This isn't getting us anywhere,' she said.

'Oh, I don't know about that.' And she noticed that his eyes had strayed to the beads of perspiration that had gathered in the little crevice between her breasts.

'Keep your eyes on the job, buddy,' she warned.

'I'd better look under the bonnet,' he said, adding hastily, 'Not your bonnet, before you go off on one again. The van's bonnet.'

'I knew what you meant,' Sam insisted but as he leaned over to look at the engine and the various leads and plugs, her eyes lingered on the way the fabric of his shorts strained over his taut physique. What was it about a man wearing tight shorts?

'Nice bum,' she murmured under her breath.

'I heard that,' he muttered. 'Now who's being sexist? Turn the key for me, will you? In the ignition,' he added slowly, as if talking to an idiot.

She flicked the key, but the engine was still dead.

'Something must have become disconnected.' He fiddled with a few wires, without success. 'Looks like we really are stuck here,' he said, shutting the bonnet with a sigh of resignation.

By now, Sam's throat felt as if it was on fire. 'I'm parched,' she said. 'Do you have anything to drink? Water? Tea, even?'

'There's a can of Coke in the glovebox,' he said, straightening up.

As she leaned over the passenger seat, Sam felt her short denim skirt move up her thighs.

'Nice bum,' he murmured.

She smiled. 'I suppose we're about even now.'

He smiled back, showing neat, white teeth.

Sam took a swig of the Coke, gulping so greedily that a jet of the fizzy brown liquid dripped down her chin and neck, splashing on her halter-neck top.

'You've spilled it,' he remarked, not taking his eyes off her.

'I don't care. I really needed that.'

'When you've finished, I'd like to quench my thirst too,' he said.

She handed him the half-drained can of Coke but instead of taking it from her, he gripped her wrist, pulling

146

her towards him. Their hot bodies collided, flesh on flesh. Sam gasped as he dipped his head, licked the sticky coke from her neck, her chin, around her lips.

'That tastes good,' he said, waiting to see how she would react. Perhaps he expected a slap round the face or a kick in the groin. He was grinning, baiting her. But it was his turn to be surprised when she grabbed the bulge in his shorts and squeezed.

'Does it taste as good as this?' she asked.

'You could always try it and see,' he suggested.

Who was calling whose bluff? Sam hesitated but one look at those mocking blue eyes decided her. She would wipe that smile off his smug face.

'All righty.' Roughly, Sam unzipped his flies and took hold of the already plump cock that was straining for release. As she brought her lips to the glistening tip, she felt it stiffen further in her firm grasp.

'Bloody hell,' he exclaimed as she sucked so hard that his eyes watered.

'Want me to stop?' she asked, lifting her head curiously.

'No, yes, no,' he groaned.

'Make your mind up.'

'No,' he confirmed.

'No, you won't make your mind up, or no, you don't want me to stop?'

'Suck me dry, you bitch,' he groaned, pushing her head down again.

She gave him a thorough working over, using her tongue and lips on the tip, the shaft, grazing her teeth on the flesh that was both tender and hard at the same time. The pent up frustrations of the past hour were at last finding release and his cock was the lucky recipient.

After a while, he grabbed a handful of Sam's hair,

yanked her head back, and said, grinning broadly, 'I think you need a good seeing to, girlie.'

Putting his hands around her waist, he lifted her into the air and threw her across the bonnet of the van.

'Christ, that's hot,' she yelped as the heat from the sun-soaked metal burnt into her flesh.

'Not as hot as your pussy will be,' he retorted, pushing her skirt up around her hips and spreading her legs wide. As Sam lay sprawled across the bonnet, he buried his face between her thighs, and she trembled as she felt his tongue expertly explore her wet pussy. She writhed, trapped between the heat of the metal and the heat between her legs as he lapped greedily. She didn't care if anyone saw her like this. All she cared about was satisfying her immediate needs – for pleasure and the resolution of that pleasure. As her arms flailed, desperate for something to hang on to as she edged closer to her goal, he grabbed her wrists with his right hand and pinned them down above her head.

'Screw you,' she panted, her breathing erratic.

He lifted his head. 'Screw you, too,' he whispered, running his free hand over her breasts, squeezing the hard, brown nipples. 'And I'm going to.'

Then he was on top of her, pushing inside, stretching her, plunging into her welcoming depths. But it wasn't enough and she wrapped her legs around his broad back, pulling him further and deeper inside her. She swore and cursed at him while running her painted fingernails down his back, under his vest, carving red lines into the sunburnt flesh. In return, his mouth fell on her lips, her neck, her shoulders with an urgent passion, kissing, biting, devouring. He serviced her with short, deep thrusts, holding her firmly in position. Their bodies were slippery from sweat and Sam thought they would both melt in the fiery heat.

'Bastard,' she screamed as she came the first time.

As she exploded, he continued to ram her harder, and she quickly felt herself on the edge once more. She was vaguely aware of car horns blaring loudly somewhere in the background but they couldn't compete with her screams of pleasure.

'Typical woman, won't shut up,' he grunted, pumping into her energetically.

'Oi! you two sex maniacs,' yelled an angry voice in the distance. 'Get out of the way. I've got a delivery to make.'

'Not until I've made my delivery,' said Sam's jousting partner, shooting his load at last.

'Typical man,' she murmured, coming again.

# Santa's Big Helper
## by Lynn Lake

I showed up for my first night of elf duty just as the chain holding back the screaming horde of kids from Santa's Winter Wonderland was lifted. The mob of SC-worshippers quickly trampled the plastic Rudolph's and Styrofoam Frosties in their headlong rush to throw themselves onto the plush velvet lap of Mr Claus. And my somewhat tardy arrival didn't go over well with less-than-jolly old Saint Nick.

"Where the hell … heck have you been!?" Father Christmas yelled at me as another elf escorted a hyperactive three-year-old out of his mother's arms and up and onto the Promised Land. "You should be here at least fifteen minutes before we open for business!"

"Sorry," I soothed the throned demigod, as I scratched my elfin headgear with my middle finger. "I guess you've never tried to spoon yourself into a costume three sizes too small."

He gave my stretched-tight holiday attire an appraising glance, his twinkling eyes lingering an inappropriately long time on my bountiful breasts, until the sucrose-charged kid with the inch-thick want list pulled his beard like it was Mommy's chain. "You are a big girl, all right," Santa said to me, ignoring the excited whisker-tugger, his voice hitting depths Barry White used to call home.

I one-finger adjusted my green, felt cap and red feather for a second time, then turned my back on his hearty leer. The last thing I needed to go along with a polar Green Giant job was a randy Claus. After getting laid off from my regular job, breaking up with my girlfriend, and putting my cat, Senor Whiskas, to sleep, I'd only just recently begun to rebuild my shattered life by snagging a couple of part-time jobs and picking up Senor Whiskas, Jr. from a neighbour whose cat had littered. Christmas was only two weeks away, and I was determined to make it a white, as opposed to blue, holiday.

The gushing stream of babbling boys and girls dwindled down to a sticky trickle as the evening wore on, providing me an opportunity to get better acquainted with my fellow merry-makers. My elf-mate, Brandi Gilky, was a teenaged chain-smoker with a set of horse teeth wrapped up in the kind of braces I thought they'd outlawed with the iron mask. Her job was to lead the little lambs from parent to Pere Noel, but even that simple task proved difficult for the high school equivalency grad, as she was more often than not chatting up the packs of aimless boys who circled the decorated mall like hammerhead sharks circle a school of tuna. Or she was running off to the bathroom to do God's knows what, or who, leaving me pulling double-duty as greeter and retriever – steering the chattering tykes in and out with a minimum of free candy and tears. Still, the girl had a cute butt and a pair of nipples that dimpled her vest in a most appealing manner, so she wasn't all bad.

Santa, on the other hand, wasn't all good. He was a short little guy with a deep voice, blue eyes, and roving hands. He was sporting enough padding to fill a living room set, and when he wasn't two-fisting coffee, he was patting my costumed epidermis like he worked airport security. The dolly-jolly old coot was constantly caressing my hand or arm, or squeezing my elbow, whenever I came to collect his toy-seeking cargo. I figured that either Mrs Claus was an icicle, or that Santa wasn't shy about stuffing his stocking whenever and wherever he could, because the sawed-off Christmas icon was as horny as a Salvation Army brass band.

I didn't mind his light-fingered, white-fingered pawing so much, but when the crowds really started to thin out, in prelude to mall-closing, he started blatantly groping me – patting my hip, rubbing my thigh, goosing me. Now, that was too much. "You and me are gonna have a little talk at ten o'clock," I told the lecherous pole-dweller.

"Just a talk?" he rumbled, his eyes gleaming as he fondled the oversized belt buckle that no doubt compensated for an undersized Yule log.

I handed him a glare that would've frosted most men's chestnuts, and finished out my shift in chilly silence. And when the candy-cane clock finally struck ten, and buttalicious Brandi with the braces re-chained the entrance to kiddy nirvana, I grabbed the crimson-clad lothario by the arm, pulled him onto his booties, and shoved him inside Santa's snow-painted workshop.

"Okay, bub," I said, shaking the chunky little ho-meister like a suspicious Christmas present, "let's get a few things straight. First of all, if you ever touch –"

I shut up when he kissed me full on the lips.

I gawked at the festive cherub like Daddy must've gawked when he caught Santa french-kissing Mommy. The guy was maybe five-foot-three, a hundred and ten pounds, while I'm almost six-feet-tall and a hundred and seventy-five pounds. It wasn't going to be a fair fight, but that was fine with me; he hadn't treated me fair all night. "Okay, you asked for it," I snarled, pulling back my fist.

He held up his hands, started laughing. "Wait a minute, Joy! Don't you recognize me?"

"Yeah," I responded, nodding, my big fist quivering like a bow-flexed arrow. "I recognize your type."

He chortled some more, then said in a voice gone from gong to bell, "It's me, Joy! Sandra!" She pulled off her wig and beard.

My arm dropped to my side and my eyes widened. I unscruffed her collar and gasped, "Sandra!?"

"Yes, it's me, you big lunk." She peeled off her gloves and coat, and then quickly stripped away her boots, pants, and padding, and stood in front of me in nothing more constraining than a black bra and panties.

Wow! She had unwrapped one hell of a Christmas present! My incredulous eyes flew up and down her hot body, landing briefly on her pussy and tits, while memories stirred in my head like a mouse on the night before the night before Christmas. Sandra and I had gone out a number of times two years previously, before she'd moved to another city, and during those dates I had discovered depths to my want, heights to my passion, and intensities of orgasm that I'd never thought existed before. And with those sugar-plum sweet visions dancing in my dizzy head, I eyed the sexy blonde babe and licked my dry lips with a wooden tongue. "You're back in town?" I whispered.

"What does it look like?" she replied, blushing under my heated stare. She plucked out some hair pins and ran her slender fingers through her long, silky tresses. "Things weren't working out, so I quit my job and moved

153

back here about a month ago. I just took this Santa gig to earn some extra money." She grinned. "I'm quite the actress, don't you think?" she said, in the bottom-of-the-monkey-barrel voice that had fooled all the kids, and yours truly.

"I don't wanna think," I muttered, and grabbed the tiny honey in my arms and crushed my lips against hers.

"Yes, Joy, yes," she breathed into my mouth, her erect nipples pressing urgently into my soft breasts.

We kissed long and hard and hungrily in the cramped, shadowed confines of Santa's sweatshop, and then I parted her full-bodied lips with my slippery pink spear and we frenched each other. It had been much too long for both of us, and we savagely took up where we'd left off a couple of years ago, swirling our tongues together in a ferociously erotic ballet.

She broke away from my mouth and said, "Shouldn't we, uh … shouldn't we find a more, um, comfortable spot for our reunion?"

"What better place to be naughty?" I responded with a wicked smile, knowing that my overpowering desire demanded to be quelled right then and there. I tore off my elfish duds like they were blazing with chimney fire, and then more slowly and sensuously slid my panties over my big, round butt and popped open my bulging bra. My snow-white breasts spilled out into the open in an avalanche of flesh, and my ultra-pink nipples peaked at full one-inch hardness in the humid, super-heated air. My pussy was moist and raw, aching for fingers and tongue.

"You put the hour in hour-glass figure, baby," Sandra said, staring admiringly at my over-ripe body and reaching up to stroke my short, black hair. She then cast aside her own undergarments, along with her inhibitions, and we passionately embraced again, our nude, lewd, flaming bodies and need threatening to reduce the faux-gingerbread house to a smoking lump of coal.

We frenched some more, then I captured Sandra's darting tongue between my teeth and began sucking it. She stuck her slimy pleasure tool as far out of her mouth as she could, and I urgently sucked up and down its wet, rigid length like someone might suck a swollen candy cane. She caressed and fondled my tits as I did so. Then the petite cutie broke away from my mouth and really went to work on my chest. She clutched my breasts, squeezed them together, and teased my sensitive buds with her playful tongue – spanking first one distended nip and then the other, swirling her tongue around my huge aureoles. Then she swallowed a nipple in her mouth and tugged on it.

"Yeah, Sandra! Suck my tits!" I shrieked, my lust-addled voice booming out joy to the world.

The faint whir of floor-buffing machines could be heard after the echoes of my screams had died down, as the mall cleaning staff worked away just outside the thin walls of our sugar shack, but at that moment, and the sexually-charged moments that followed, I could have cared less if the real Claus himself had stormed down the chimney demanding milk and nookie. Sandra was working miracles on my tingling tits, sucking hard on one engorged nipple and then the other, bobbing her blonde head back and forth between my boobs, cheeks billowing, breath steaming out of her flared nostrils as she greedily fed on my tits.

"God, that feels good," I groaned, as she kneaded and tongued my Christmas mams.

She looked up at me, her eyes wild, her hands and mouth full of titty, and she asked, "Can you still handle the vertical sixty-nine, baby?"

I stroked her golden hair with trembling fingers, closed my eyes while she painted my glistening nipples with her hot saliva. "For you, sweetie, I think I can summon the strength," I murmured.

And with that assurance, she jumped into my arms and wrapped her legs around my waist. I opened my eyes and set myself, then carefully manoeuvred the gorgeous, light-as-feather hottie around until I was facing her delightfully drenched blonde pussy. I held her easily, shouldering her smooth, supple legs as she coiled them about my neck. She wasted no time in spreading my pussy lips and plunging two fingers inside my burning snatch.

"Fuck, yeah!" I yelped, my knees buckling as the anxious girl frantically finger-fucked me, as she probed my clit with her warm, wet tongue. I gripped her taut little ass cheeks, breathed in her moist, musky scent for a couple of ticks, and then drove my tongue into her pussy.

"Yes, Joy! Eat me!" she squealed, hammering her fingers in and out of my soaking wet pussy, buffing my swollen clitty with her tongue.

I felt a wave of incredible heat rise like a fiery tide up my quivering body, and I knew that devastating orgasm was not far away. I lapped at her smoldering twat, tongue-stroking her from clit to butthole in long, sensuous strokes. She squirmed in my arms, but I held on tight, never wanting to let go, ever again. Then I latched onto the girl's pink, protruding nub with my lips and sucked for all I was worth.

"I'm cumming!" she screamed, even as she desperately ploughed my pussy with her fingers, polished my electrified clit with her thumb.

She let out a high-pitched, almost inaudible moan and

spasmed uncontrollably as an orgasm exploded inside of her. She was jolted again and again with ecstasy, as orgasm after orgasm thundered through her, shattering body and soul.

I quickly joined her in our rediscovered sexual utopia. "Merry fucking Christmas!" I bellowed, as a searing orgasm churned through my quaking body, rapidly followed by another, and another. I blindly struggled to tongue up Sandra's scalding girl juices as she came over and over, as she sent my own senses skyrocketing into the blissful clouds of ecstasy with her unrelenting fingers.

Finally, when the roof had settled back down on our fantasyland fuckhouse, I weakly turned Sandra around and put her back on her feet. We kissed and licked each other's sugar-coated lips, tasting our own cumdrops as we fiercely hugged one another. And it wasn't the twelve days of Christmas I was looking forward to now, but rather the twelve nights.

# Butterscotch Drops And Caramel Cups
## by Izzy French

The moment Mr Bembridge went out the back to replenish the strawberry bonbons I closed my eyes, stretched out my arms and breathed in deeply. The moment felt sensual. Bembridge's Sweetshop had always made me shiver with excitement, even when I'd been a small child, but I'd only recently felt positively turned on by being there. I kept this to myself of course. It was my guilty secret. Who else in this world could find a sweetshop sexy? The sharpness of acid drops made my nose itch. When I licked my lips I could tasted the smooth creaminess of butterscotch. My hands reached for the liquorice laces displayed in the scoop on the counter. Slowly my fingertips unravelled the coil, and I allowed the laces to escape the tangle and drop one by one to the counter. I could hardly believe I would be paid, one week in arrears, one month's probation, to work in my own personal heaven.

"A quarter of aniseed drops, please miss," a voice whispered. Startled, I opened my eyes and my hands threw the remaining laces to the floor, causing them to skitter across the wood like eels unexpectedly released from capture.

"Of course, sir." My eyes scanned the dozens of glass

jars surrounding me. I couldn't focus. Was this a test? Would I fail on my first day, and be asked to leave, my dream over before it had begun? Of course, as a customer, I would have been able to point to aniseed drops in the dark, though I never bought them. I considered them old men's sweets. And it was an old man who stood in front of me, at first looking expectant, now beginning to look a little impatient.

"They're up there in the corner, Lucy." Mr Bembridge saved me. I glanced at him. At first his face looked stern, then he broke into a grin.

"Think we need to set some time aside for training. It's not fair to drop you in at the deep end. Perhaps you could stay on after we close. I could help get you more acquainted with the range and positioning of the stock. I'll give you a chance to taste some too. It'll help you recommend things to the customers when they come in fancying a change, which they often do."

"Of course, Mr Bembridge. That's fine," I replied.

"And don't worry, Lucy, you're a natural, a kindred spirit." He rested his hand on my shoulder for a moment, and gave it a brief rub. I felt the tension ease from my back. But I still hesitated before climbing the stepladders to reach the aniseed drops. The skirt I was wearing was fashionably short and my legs were bare. I was short too, though less fashionably so. I was certain that, when I reached for the aniseed drops, the elderly customer and Mr Bembridge would catch a glimpse of my 'Love is …' knickers. I climbed the ladders carefully, pulled the jar towards me and descended the steps. Before I turned to face the customer I heard a sharp release of breath. I blushed and shook the aniseed drops into the scales, then into a crisp white paper bag and handed them over, avoiding his eye.

159

"That'll be six pence, please." I finally looked up after I'd rung the amount into the till. The customer was grinning at me. I looked at Mr Bembridge. He was busy filling the strawberry bonbon jar. He gave me an encouraging nod. I returned the customer's smile and handed him his change. He gave me a wink as he turned to leave. The rest of the day flew by in a blur. I served old dears with a quarter of pear drops, mums and children after school, and men in suits on their way home, newspapers tucked under their arms. I felt worn out when Mr Bembridge finally rolled down the shutters and turned the key in the lock.

"You did well today, Lucy," he said as he pulled two stools up behind the counter. "It was a bit of a baptism of fire. It's been so long since I've had an assistant, afraid I left you on your own a bit too much. Have a rest for a few minutes. I'll be back with you in a moment." He disappeared behind the plastic curtain into the stock room. I turned and rested my elbows on the long oak counter. I'd always liked Mr Bembridge when I came into the shop as a customer. I'd drop in late afternoon, carefully counting the coins in my purse, trying to work out which was best value, a quarter of barley sugars or liquorice toffee. And Mr Bembridge was kind.

"Oops," he'd say as the scales tipped well over the quarter mark.

"Never mind, not worth putting them back now. You might as well have them."

He'd told me about the vacancy for an assistant, encouraged me to apply. And he was quite fanciable too, even though he was a few years older than me. He had deep brown eyes, a nice smile and floppy hair.

"Call me Paul, by the way, we're colleagues now." His voice startled me. "Here you go." He was carrying two large glass jars and a long hand-written list. I didn't think I could call him Paul. Not yet.

"This is our stock list. Sometimes people will ask you for a recommendation. To suit their mood, maybe. So you'll need to know what all the sweets taste like, as well as their names. You know what it's like, when you come into the shop you think you'll try something different. But then when you're faced with rows and rows of jars to choose from you tend to go for the old favourites. We want to shake our customers out of that habit."

He moved his stool close to mine and reached for the first jar.

"I know one of your personal favourites is strawberry bonbons."

I nodded.

"Take one and tell me about it. Why do you like them?"

I gulped, hoping Mr Bembridge's expectations weren't going to be too high. I reached into the first jar and pulled out a strawberry bonbon. He took one too. When I placed it in my mouth I remembered immediately why I liked them so much.

"It's that slight crunch, followed by chewiness and that sweet strawberry flavour. It's the perfect combination. Mmmm."

The sweet had left a dusting of strawberry-flavour sugar on my lips. Mr Bembridge brushed it away with the tip of his finger. His touch was light, and it left a tingling sensation on my lips. I gasped, surprised at his touch. He leant forward and gave me the softest kiss imaginable.

"You taste of strawberries," he smiled as he pulled away. "And an excellent, succinct description. Couldn't do better myself." He reached for the next jar. I squirmed on the stool enjoying the warm feeling between my legs

161

as I pressed them together. The feeling was so sweet I wanted to reach down and touch, but I kept my hands resting in my lap, for now.

"Let's try sherbets next. Not a sweet you ever buy, is it Lucy?"

I shook my head. I found sherbets tangy, fizzy. Wake you up sweets.

"No, but I'll give them a try."

"Close your eyes, please. And open your mouth."

The sensation of sherbet on my tongue was intense, as I expected. But not as intense as the kiss Mr Bembridge followed it with. His lips pressed against mine, and I returned his kiss. This was good. I was enjoying sherbet. Our tongues moved together, the sherbet fizzing between them. After a few long and delicious moments Mr Bembridge pulled away from me.

"Sharp and sweet," I whispered, describing the sherbet and the kiss.

"You're doing well, Lucy. You're a quick learner. Well done."

Next came butterscotch drops. We both sucked on one. As we did so he unbuttoned my blouse and released the clasp of my bra. And I let him. In fact, I helped him, pulling my blouse from my shoulders and dropping it to the floor along with my bra. Strange, now I was half naked I didn't feel exposed. Just good. Mr Bembridge stood in front of me now, right close up. He leant and licked my left breast, the butterscotch drop still in his mouth, massaging my right breast with his hand. The feeling was sensational. My eyes closed and I surrendered to the pleasure. My nipple tightened as he took it between his lips, rolled and nipped it, tugged it gently. I moaned in delight. Sex and sweets go together well.

"Melt slowly in the mouth, creamy and smooth," I said as he pulled away. He nodded his approval and rubbed his hand along my thigh and under my skirt, pressing it against my mound. I parted my legs, inviting him to explore further.

"I'd like a caramel cup, now Lucy. Perhaps you could fetch the jar down for me."

The caramel cups were on the top shelf behind us. I pulled the heavy wooden steps over and began to climb. As I reached for the jar, my breasts raised. I could tell they looked good. And from the way Mr Bembridge was caressing and holding them I imagined they felt good too. It was his turn to groan. I took one step down, the jar in my hands, and I felt him stop me. His fingers sent a bolt through me as they moved up the back of my legs, his touch light. I placed the jar on the top of the steps, and leant forward, ensuring my arse was closer to his face. Now it was my turn to hold my breasts. Pinching and twisting my nipples I felt the pressure of his hands increase as he reached the tops of my thighs. With one hand he pulled my knickers down and helped me steady myself as I stepped out of them. The fingers of his other hand ran down between my buttocks and into my slit. I shuffled around, offering him the best possible access. This felt good already. I wanted it to be perfect.

A hard rap on the door interrupted our pleasure, but only momentarily. I could see the outline of a customer through the blinds. I turned to Mr Bembridge and gave him a questioning look. Should we stop? He shook his head and put a finger to his lips. His other hand was exploring me, and it wasn't easy now to keep quiet, my pleasure was mounting towards climax. His fingers thrust into my cunt, and my juices eased their passage. Then they rubbed my clit, softly and slowly to begin with, building up a wonderful rhythm. He pulled away and parted my legs further. This time his tongue licked and sucked my cunt, lapping up my juices, encircling my clit and working me into a frenzy. I wanted to come right now, to feel the waves of pleasure course through me. But he pulled away just moments before my climax came. I knew he wasn't going to disappoint me, though, not now. Not as we'd come so far.

"Could you turn round, Lucy." His voice was soft. "I love caramel cups," he whispered. "They melt in your mouth." His lips glistened. He leant forward again to bury his face in me once more, before lifting me and placing me in a sitting position on the counter. I parted my legs. I wanted more of him. I reached for my clit, gently rubbing it, keeping myself close in anticipation of what was coming next.

"Chocolate, now I think. Buttons maybe. Lean back a little."

I complied. He was my boss, after all. He picked up a handful of buttons from a scoop to his right and rested a few on my mound. The heat of my body soon began to melt them, and the trickle of chocolate over my clit was the sweetest sensation imaginable. Until I felt his tongue devour the liquid. Then I was in ecstasy. I needed him to fuck me now.

"I think it's time to move on to the next level of training, Lucy." Quickly he loosened his trousers and tugged his underpants away, exposing his erect cock. It was beautiful and I was ready for him. The counter was at perfect cock height. I pulled myself to the edge, and offered him my throbbing pussy. He pushed his way in, slowly and gently at first. We were a perfect fit, and as I tensed around him he began to thrust. I held on to the counter to push against him and we built up a rhythm.

His fingers and mine found my clit, and matched the rhythm of our fucking. Now there was no going back from my climax, and as the waves of my pleasure tightened around him I felt him groan as he filled me.

"What a sweet fuck," he said a few moments later, as he began to recover. I pulled his lips to mine and kissed him.

"Sweet, indeed."

"You've made excellent progress today, Lucy. I'm sure we'll work well together, you and I," he said as I pulled my clothes on. Licking my lips I could still taste chocolate and strawberry bonbons.

"I think we'll try some tasting with the aid of a blindfold after work tomorrow," he added, as I was about to leave. "If that's OK with you? Maybe see if we can find new uses for liquorice laces."

Working in a sweet shop is tiring, but such fun, I thought, as I walked home. I sucked slowly at the candy cane Mr Bembridge had given me as he kissed me goodbye.

# Kiss And Tell
## by Mimi Elise

We were watching the Awards when the camera cut to him. He sat among the audience with a beautiful blonde at his side. When he realised the camera was on him, he smiled that languid smile. The smile that set a million female hearts racing, when they weren't admiring his toned body.

"Here we go," said Babs. "Cassie will start in a minute. The ultimate kiss and tell."

"I knew him before he was famous," said Vicky, mimicking my voice. "He said he'd thank me when he got an Oscar."

"I made a man of him," said Babs, joining in. "He was a virgin till he met me." I hadn't told them that!

"If you slept with Jonathon Grant, why haven't you sold the story to the newspapers?" said Vicky. "I know I would if I'd had a celebrity. I can just see you, on the front page of *The News of the World*, wearing a push up bra, with the headline 'Jonathon Granted All My Wishes'."

"Yes, how big was his magic wand again?" asked Babs.

"Oh, shut up," I said, pulling a cushion up to my reddened cheeks. I sometimes wish I'd never said anything to them. It's amazing how you can pull any washed-up bloke at the club on a Saturday night and everyone believes you. Spend a divine hour with someone gorgeous who later becomes a superstar and they think you're deluded.

Unable to bear my friends' teasing, I got up and went into my bedroom. I flicked the television on just as they were announcing the nominations for best supporting actor. He was among the nominees. What I'd told my friends was the truth. I did know him before he was famous. Before the stylists got to him; before he affected the trans-Atlantic drawl; before his jack-the-lad lifestyle in Hollywood got him into all the gossip columns; before he met the stick insect that the same gossip columns said he'd soon marry. It was fair to say he'd embraced stardom, and all that it brought him. He'd also embraced a lot of women. Chances are I was just another notch on the bedpost.

Five years before it had been a different story. He played the starring role in a Shakespeare production at a small theatre in my hometown and I was the cub reporter sent to interview him. He'd been hailed as the man most likely to succeed by his drama school, and was due to appear in an expensive BBC costume drama, which by all accounts involved him spending very little time in a costume of any kind. It would be his groundbreaking role, but when I met him he'd only played a few bit parts, such as a villain in The Bill and a patient with an unusual disease in Casualty.

We met in his dressing room. The moment I saw him, I knew he was movie star material. A little rough around the edges perhaps, dressed in jeans and a creased white shirt, with the beginnings of a five o'clock shadow on his chin. But he was also beautiful with vivid green eyes under perfectly arched dark brows. He was tall too. There'd be no standing on a box to reach the leading lady for him. He leaned back on the sofa, while I perched on the arm of the chair, finding it impossible to relax in the company of such perfection. I was all too aware of the sweater I'd thrown on that morning over a skirt that suddenly felt very short.

"I see my future as playing a selection of evil Englishmen in American films," he said in answer to my question. His voice was deep, like thick, melted chocolate. I had a bit of a thing about baddies, and told him so.

"As long as they only kill other bad people," I added for good measure. I stopped short of telling him that Alan Rickman in *Die Hard* was my favourite fantasy. I'd begun to realise that the divine Alan might be usurped.

"And they have to be kind to their lady loves, I suppose," he said.

"Absolutely."

"And give her mind-blowing sex."

I didn't know how to answer that other than with the affirmative. He looked me up and down, causing me to wriggle on the arm of my chair. My panties felt damp beneath me. I knew that the moment this man appeared on the big screen he'd be the catalyst for a million female orgasms. He wasn't doing too badly with just me in the room.

"Mind-blowing sex is compulsory, especially for bad guys," I said before I could stop myself. "They have a lot of naughtiness to make up for."

"I'll bear that in mind when I get my first role. Do you think I should start practising now?"

"It's probably wise to be prepared. Even if you're only going to be faking it." I felt I had to get the conversation back on to reality and not the fantasies that were rushing through my head of us playing out every film sex scene I'd ever watched. Nine and a half weeks could easily become a year if only he'd give me the opportunity.

Feeling flustered, and realising I had no more questions for him, I stood up and started to say my goodbyes. He stood up too. Standing closer to me, he reached down and kissed my cheek.

"Goodbye, Cassie," he said. "When I get my Oscar I'll thank you for taking an interest in a nobody." His lips moved to my mouth, where they rested lightly. I had the feeling he was testing me to see if I responded.

I tilted my head to kiss him back, pretending to myself that it would be a quick peck. It was all the encouragement he needed. His lips possessed mine, his tongue sliding into my partly open mouth while his arms encircled my waist. One hand slid down to my rear, pulling up my skirt and cupping one buttock, while his fingers slipped between my thighs, lifting me to him. His erection pressed against my belly. My groin ached with longing. I wasn't known for being easy but for him I made an exception. After all, he'd hardly be bragging about me down at the pub with his mates. Why not enjoy one day of fantastic sex with him before all those starlets got their hands on him?

I don't remember how we got out of our clothes; I just knew that a few minutes later we lay on the tiny sofa, our clothes strewn around the room where we'd frantically discarded them. His well-toned body covered mine, making me feel small and vulnerable. One hand caressed my breast, bringing it up to his mouth. He ran his tongue around my nipple, then took it all into his mouth, pulling the nipple outwards until it stood erect, and causing a sensation that ran all the way down to my sex. I scraped my nails lightly down his back to his buttocks, digging into the fleshy mounds as he increased the pressure on my breast. He really did have the nicest bum I'd ever been privileged to caress.

He trailed kisses down my belly, pulling my legs apart as he knelt on the floor. At first he just looked at my sex, parting it with his fingers. It made me feel shy, but also very turned on while he watched the effects his probing fingers had on my vulva. I could tell it aroused him too. His eyes glittered and he licked his lips as though looking at a meal he'd yet to taste. I could feel his breath tickling my pubic hair. His head swooped and his warm, wet tongue found me. I cried out as an unexpected jolt of pleasure burst through my body. He searched out my clit, moving his tongue faster, while his hand reached up and caressed my breast. I put my own hand over it, urging him to squeeze harder. His fingers, his tongue, he used them all to pleasure me, until at last my body, trembling and exhausted gave into the sensations. I came into his mouth.

In the confusion of the orgasm, I felt him move away and wondered, sadly, if that was it. I looked up to see him putting on a condom.

"I wanted to suck you," I said.

"This is your wish, Cassie," he replied. "Come here."

I stood up, my knees still trembling. He clasped my hands and pulled me to the floor. He moved into a sitting position, then placed my legs either side of him, pulling me closer. We sat facing, our crotches touching. Once again his fingers found my vulva, while we kissed deep and long. His hands slid under my buttocks and he guided me onto his cock. I felt him fill me, but the position meant we couldn't move much.

"Oh please," I said. "Harder." He kissed me and

stroked my hair.

"Shhh," he whispered. "Trust me." Still we rocked together. I wanted him to throw me back and fuck me senseless, but he was in control and soon I began to realise why. The gentle rocking caused his cock to press against a pleasure point deep inside me. It was like a deep heat, pulling at me, building slowly. The gentle motion caused our whole bodies to slide together as a fine mist of perspiration covered us both. The hairs on his chest tickled me, while his strong thighs pressed against my lower back. Soon the heat inside me began to grow, and I struggled to move faster against his hips. He still kept the pace, gripping me hard against him. The smile on his face told me he was teasing me.

"No!" I said, pushing him onto his back, so I finally sat astride him. I pushed down hard onto his cock, and he cried out. Slamming against him, I gained the speed I'd longed for, fucking him as hard as I'd wanted him to fuck me. My long hair fell onto his chest, and he clutched a handful, pressing it to his mouth. I felt his cock twitching inside me, as he tried to stem his orgasm, so I moved faster still, until he could fight it no more. We came together, in an explosion of pleasure that left us both breathless and exhausted.

Ten minutes later, I got my breath back, while he lay on the sofa naked, with his eyes closed. I kneeled near to him and gently ran my tongue along the tip of his cock. He groaned, and put his hands in my hair. "I said this was your day," he murmured, but didn't stop me.

"Just one more wish," I said, before taking him fully into my mouth.

And that was the only time I ever met him. And my friends didn't believe me.

I watched the television as they called him to collect

his award. Jonathon was still so gorgeous, oozing the sex appeal that had left me breathless. He thanked a whole list of people and began to walk away from the pedestal. He'd probably completely forgotten me. Then something happened. He walked back to the pedestal, surprising the comedian who was presenting the show.

"I don't usually kiss and tell but I just remembered a promise I once made after one of the best afternoons I ever spent," he said in his proper voice, devoid of the trans-Atlantic accent. "I have to say thanks to Cassie."

I fell back on the bed, elated, as several pairs of footsteps thundered towards the bedroom.

"Call *The News of the World*! Get Max Clifford on the phone!" said Babs.

I knew this was one kiss and tell I'd be keeping to myself. It was time to do a follow-up interview. If Jonathon remembered me after all this time, he might be willing to grant me another wish.

# Private Lessons
## by Kristina Wright

I looked at the door in front of me. It sported three stickers with the names of heavy metal bands I vaguely recognized and a jockstrap hanging rather forlornly from the doorknob. It was, I decided, the low point in my life to be standing at that door.

The problem with returning to college at the age of forty is that everywhere I look, I see someone who could be my kid. This is not a good thing. I don't know when or how forty snuck up on me, but it did. I don't look forty, but more importantly, I don't feel forty. It doesn't matter, though. I'm forty and that means half of the students on campus are young enough to be my children. Okay, maybe even more than half.

Being a graduate student only helps a little. True, a lot of people in graduate programs are older – there are even a few who are older than me – but with the new accelerated programs, there are plenty of kids in my classes. Kids who just started drinking legally and who think "I Love the 80s" is cool because it's so retro. Truth is, I don't usually mind being the oldest chick in the room. I get along better with people who are younger than me, but it's hard to keep up with the slang, never mind the technology, and sometimes I feel my age.

It was a computer project that was kicking my ass. I can write a twenty-page paper, no problem, but tell me to do something with computer-based presentation and I'm like a deer in headlights. My son Charlie is always after me to take a class at the local library, but I'm getting my M.A. in English, not engineering, so I figured I could muddle through with the basics of word processing. That was until I got an English professor who wanted us to "think outside the box" and create a multimedia presentation.

I got married young, while I was still an undergrad, and had Charlie right away. His dad took off when Charlie was four, so it had always been the two of us and I usually felt pretty young and cool, the ubiquitous single mother doing her thing. Now, facing the complications of computer software, I was definitely feeling my age. Unfortunately, Charlie was several thousand miles away doing a semester abroad in China, leaving me alone to figure things out on my own.

My professor, a woman who was probably five years younger than me, had given me the number of her teaching assistant. Matthew Wheaton was apparently not only an excellent English Literature student, he was a whiz with computers. He also sounded like he was twelve years old on the phone, which made me feel like an even bigger idiot.

So there I was, nervously knocking on the door of Matthew's off-campus apartment and vowing to take a computer class over the summer, when someone spoke behind me.

"Sorry, I ran out for some stuff and it took longer than I thought."

I jumped and spun, nearly stumbling. I recognized Matthew from around campus, he had the boyish good looks of a college nerd who didn't realize his charm. He wore battered jeans with rips at the knees and a T-shirt of one of the bands on the door. He smiled crookedly and my heart started hammering in my chest like some adolescent girl with a crush. I pulled myself together and tried to act my age.

"Hey," I said, sounding like a croaking frog.

"You're Andrea, right?"

"Oh, right. Sorry." Sweet young Matthew had me stumbling over myself and we weren't even in his apartment yet. "Dr Hanover said you'd be able to help me with this presentation."

He manoeuvred past me and opened the door to his apartment, tossing the wayward jockstrap inside. "My roommate's idea of a joke. Laundry day," he said, by way of an explanation. "Come on in."

I'd raised a teenage boy, so I was expecting the worst, but Matthew wasn't so bad. It was a small apartment and, judging by the laundry basket by the door with women's underwear folded neatly on top, I assumed his roommate was a girl. The place smelled like pizza and pot and the furniture was old and worn, but for the most part it looked sanitary.

Matthew went into the kitchen, which was little more than an alcove with the basics, while I stood awkwardly by the door, waiting for him to put away his groceries. Like most college-age guys, his groceries consisted mostly of potato chips, sandwich stuff and beer, with granola bars, a bottle of juice and some fruit thrown in for good measure. He kept glancing up at me and smiling and I fidgeted nervously, contemplating taking an incomplete in the English class just so I could get out of there.

Matthew screwed up his shopping bags and shoved

them into a paper bag by the refrigerator. When he bent over, I could see the white band of his underwear above his low-slung jeans. "Okay. Now we can get to work."

I looked around the apartment, spotting the television, stereo and gaming system, but not seeing a computer. "Um ... where?"

Carrying two beers, Matthew headed down the hall. "My room."

I'm glad he wasn't looking at me, because I was pretty sure my eyes were bugging out of my head. I had no idea what the hell was wrong with me and as I followed Matthew down the short hall, trying not to notice his cute butt, I chastised myself. I was old enough to be his mother, for heaven's sake! Somehow, whatever mechanism controls the libido wasn't buying the old lady lecture. I felt young – and horny. I did some mental maths and figured out it had been nine months since I'd got laid, so it was no wonder I was itching to get into Matthew's bedroom for more than tutoring. But still, this was definitely the wrong place at the wrong time.

"Crash anywhere you want and I'll boot up my computer," Matthew said, dropping into his desk chair, which happened to be the only chair in the room.

I looked around nervously, but there was only one place for me to sit. The bed. The king-sized bed. I perched on the edge, nearly falling off in the process, more than a little conscious of the rumpled sheets beneath me and Matthew's wide shoulders in front of me. Granted, he was hunched over his computer and not flinging me down on the mattress, but I have a good imagination. Too good, maybe.

I fixated on the way his jeans rode down when he leaned forward, revealing the top of his underwear again. Something about that line of white above the faded blue of his jeans made me squirm in my own jeans. It was, quite possibly, the sexiest thing I'd seen in a very long time.

"So, where do we need to start?"

I was so lost in my fantasy of slowly stripping sweet Matthew and discovering whether his underwear were boxers or briefs that I hadn't really been listening. "Huh?"

He looked at me over his shoulder. "Where do you want me to start?"

I could think of a few places, but I refrained from offering those suggestions. "Well, I know how to use a mouse and I know how to turn on the monitor, but beyond word processing, I'm clueless."

Matthew made a little grunting noise and nodded. "Okay. Don't worry, I'll get you up to speed."

Over the course of the next two hours and four more beers between us, Matthew was true to his word. I not only knew how to put together a computer-based multimedia presentation, I had a pretty good start on my *Frankenstein: Monster or Man* project. I also had a pretty good buzz. That's another thing about getting older: I couldn't hold my liquor any more.

I giggled and didn't even care that it didn't sound very adult-like.

Matthew gave me a sidelong glance. "Um, you OK?"

"Sure? Why?" I giggled again.

He smiled. "'Cause you sound a little drunk."

Oops. I'd been caught. I felt warm, but I couldn't tell if I was blushing or if it was just the beer raising my temperature. "I don't usually drink that much."

"You only had three beers."

"Exactly," I said. In truth, I wasn't drunk. I knew exactly where I was and exactly who I was with. And

177

exactly what I wanted to do with him. To him. "C'mere, Matthew."

He stared at me.

I patted the bed. His bed. "C'mon, I'm not drunk and I won't bite." I gave him my best 'come hither' glance, hoping it wasn't too dusty from lack of use to be effective.

Confusion turned to recognition. One minute Matthew was sitting at his desk and the next minute he was sitting next to me. "Okay, I'm here."

I smiled. Matthew smiled. I'd love to say it was the alcohol buzz that made me lean forward and kiss a man nearly half my age, but it wasn't. It was lust. His mouth tasted like beer, and mine probably did, too. His lips were warm and firm and however young he was, he definitely knew how to kiss.

At some point, Matthew decided I was wearing too many clothes and I felt him unbuttoning my shirt. I moaned when he fondled my tits, my nipples standing at attention and probably wondering what the hell was going on. He got my shirt off easily enough, but I had to help him with the bra. Apparently, he wasn't used to front clasps. I giggled and fell back on the bed, pulling him down with me.

"This is crazy," he mumbled as he kissed and nibbled his way down my neck and across my collarbone.

At least he hadn't said 'weird'. "Crazy good or crazy bad?" I whimpered when he latched onto one swollen nipple.

"Good," he said, his mouth full.

I was anxious to get things moving past second base, so I nudged his shoulder. "Hey, Matthew?"

He looked up, his eyes heavy-lidded with his own growing lust. "What? Did I do something wrong?"

Younger men are just so damned adorable. "No, I just wanted to know what kind of underwear you're wearing." To accentuate my point, I ran my finger along the elastic of his underwear.

He looked at me as if I'd asked him who his long distance provider was. "Huh?"

"Boxers? Briefs? Oh, never mind, I'll find out for myself." I reached for the waistband of his jeans and got them unfastened. The rasp of the zipper made my clit tingle. "Oh," I sighed, tugging his jeans down his legs. "Boxer briefs."

Matthew raised his hips so I could get his jeans off and reached for the waistband of his underwear.

I put my hands over his. "Wait," I whispered.

"Why?"

I spoke to his impressive erection. "Because I like your underwear."

Matthew's boxer briefs fitted him like a second skin, hugging the bulge of his swollen cock. I licked my lips. I was looking forward to seeing him naked, but I was teasing myself – and him.

"You're driving me crazy," he whispered, reaching for me.

I pulled back. "Wait." With a few awkward moves, I got my jeans and panties off and stretched out on top of him. "Mmm, that feels nice." I wiggled on him, feeling the press of his cock between my legs.

"C'mon, baby," he said.

"Not yet." That's the thing about us older chicks, we know there's plenty of time to do everything we want to do. No need to rush. "Not just yet."

I kept rubbing against him. The friction of the cotton against my clit was nearly enough to make me come. I knew I was leaving a wet spot on his underwear, but I didn't care. I kept rubbing. He pressed his hips up to meet my downward movements, anchoring his hands on my hips as I undulated against him.

As if sensing my approaching orgasm, he started thrusting against me harder. I whimpered, burying my face in his neck as my orgasm slammed into me. He kept sliding me up and down his crotch as I clung to him. I felt like I'd never stop coming and I ground myself against him, wanting something inside my throbbing cunt. Finally, my orgasm subsided and my breathing returned to normal.

"Wow," I said.

"Hell, yeah." He laughed.

I pulled away and leaned over his body, pressing my lips to his cloth-covered cock. His underwear tasted like me. His cock twitched against my mouth and seemed to swell even more, if that was possible. I traced the outline of his arousal with my tongue. Finally, I zeroed in on the head of his cock, sucking the engorged tip between my lips. He laid there, arms at his sides, eyes closed, content to let me have my way with him. I sucked him through his underwear until the cloth of his boxer briefs was soaked through and the white cotton clung to his cock.

Slowly, ever so slowly, I dragged his underwear down until his cock popped free. It was so hard and beautiful, I ached to feel it inside me. I hesitated.

Reading my mind, he pointed to the table beside the bed. "In the drawer."

I found a box of condoms and fumbled with one until I got it open. I rolled it over the tip of his cock and down the thick shaft. Lying there, with his boxer briefs pushed down to just below his ass, his heavy cock laying against his thigh, Matthew looked at me and said one word.

"Please."

I straddled his hips, guiding his thick cock inside me inch by excruciating inch until we were both panting with need. Finally, I slid all the way down on his erection and felt the slightest twinge of discomfort before raising myself up and sliding back down again. Up and down, I rode Matthew's cock until he couldn't take any more of my slow movements and quickened my pace with his hands on my hips.

"Oh God, fuck me," he groaned. And I did.

I arched my back, reaching behind me to twist my hands in his boxer briefs that had slid down his thighs. He slid his hands inward across my hipbones, his thumbs settling on my swollen clit. With every downward thrust, he rewarded me by rubbing my clit until I was riding him as hard and fast as I needed to come again.

"Yeah, that's it," he gasped.

I started coming as he thrust up into me, a combination of his cock hitting my G-spot just right and his thumbs working their magic on my clit. He threw his head back and moaned, the tendons in his neck bulging with his exertion as I rode his throbbing cock. He tried to hold me still but I kept grinding on him, milking every ounce of sensation from his cock.

Finally, I let him pull me down, my body as limp and damp as he was. He stroked my back slowly, soothing me.

I kissed the pulse in his neck and sighed. "Thanks. You're a great tutor."

"You think?"

"Oh yeah," I nodded against his chest. "You can always tell a good teacher by his underwear."

# At The Hotel
## by David Inverbrae

I am already in the hotel bedroom when you arrive. I got there in the afternoon knowing that you would be coming straight from work so I had a little time to prepare for you.

I had already texted you the room number so you came straight up and knocked on the door and I let you in. You were surprised to see me in one of the hotel's towelling robes, and as you come in I pull you to me, holding you tight against my body as we kiss. Gentle at first becoming more and more passionate as our lips and tongues tease each other, my hand on your bum over your suit skirt, pulling you against me letting you feel my hardness under the robe as your thigh slides between mine.

I help you out of your jacket and unbutton your blouse, my hand moving to the zip on the back of your skirt, you feeling it loosen and wriggling your hips to help it on its way to the floor. It is soon joined by your blouse. Standing only in your underwear and heels, our tongues frantically twist and wrap round each others as we kiss deeper and harder ... then I pull back and push open the door of the bathroom. You look inside and see the bath filled to the brim with bubbles, some

182

strategically placed candles and an ice bucket with a
bottle of wine ... and beside it one glass already poured.
You look at me and ask why only one glass and I tell you
that I thought you might need some time to relax on your
own, so you should have a nice long soak in the bath on
your own while I finish off preparing the bed for you ...

You look a little disappointed that I won't be joining
you but I give you one long kiss on the back of your neck
and tell you to take as long as you want, giving you a pat
on your bum as you go in. I leave the door open and
watch as you finish undressing. Knowing I am watching
you, you face me as you take off your bra, keeping eye
contact as your reveal your breasts to me, giggling a little
as you tease your nipples before turning round and
wiggling your bum as you slide your panties down ...
making sure that you bend right forwards to slip them off
your feet rather than just stepping out of them ...
knowing that you will be giving me a spectacular view of
your pussy and bum from behind.

You climb into the bath and take a sip of your wine as
the hot water and bubbles engulf your body ... a little
yellow duck bobbing in the water in front of you. I smile
and blow you a kiss before disappearing from the open
doorway ... you just hear my voice shouting back ...
telling you to be nice to the duck. You smile to yourself
as you take another sip of the cold wine. Your glass is
needing a top up so you take the bottle out of the ice
bucket but as you pour, some iced water drips off the
bottle onto your breast making you gasp, but you move
your position slightly so that your nipple is now clear of
the water and let the next drip fall directly onto it ... your
head falling back as you try to muffle your small groan as
your nipple responds to the icy water.

The yellow duck is bobbing about in the water and

you realise that it seems to be moving on its own accord. Curious, you pick it up and understand now … it is vibrating … a tiny floating vibrator shaped like a duck. "Thanks for the duck" you call out, and you hear me laughing through in the bedroom, then shouting back "Be gentle with it … it's only small". You start to tease your nipples with it, the sensations starting off a reaction that spreads down into your pelvis. You try to open your knees more but the hotel bath is a bit narrow, so you lift your outside foot and drape it over the edge of the bath so you can tease yourself with the duck … rubbing it slowly up and down your pussy until you hold it buzzing over your clitoris. Your lips already parting on their own, you use two fingers to help, opening yourself a little more to give better access to your little pink bud. As the feelings in your pelvis start to build you can't believe it when you hear me shout through that I am ready for you in the bedroom … almost as if I know the point you had got to.

Reluctantly you put the duck back in the water and climb out, drying yourself on the only towel there then wrapping it round you just above your breasts … just long enough to cover your bum. You bring the ice bucket and bottle with you as you come through to the bedroom unsure of what you will find. You break into a smile, the bed is covered in white fluffy towels and as you put down the wine I ask you if you are ready for your massage. You answer me by letting your towel fall to the floor and squeezing past me to the bed naked before lying down on your front on the bed. You realise that under the towels are some pillows piled up and you move yourself till they are under your belly and hips, your bum raised slightly now and you know the view I will have as you open your legs a little so I can see the smooth lips of your pussy, already open and moist. "I see you enjoyed ducky" I say, and you just wriggle your bum and whisper for me to "hurry up!!"

I start at your shoulders and you feel me spread oil on your moist skin, and as my thumbs start to work in the muscles at your shoulder blades I feel you relax into the bed. "Mmmm that oil smells nice," you say. and I tell you that it is coconut oil and has some interesting properties as well as smelling and tasting good. My hands move down your back massaging either side of your spine down to the small of your back where your bum starts, then sliding up the sides of your body, my fingertips just curling round you enough that they brush the sides of your breasts as the bulge out as you lie on them. I keep this up until I can sense your breathing changing. I move down to your legs, running my oily hands up the back of your thighs. As I do, you move your hips and part your thighs more, giving me a close-up view of your pussy from behind. The room has gone very quiet, only the sound of our breathing breaking the silence and knowing how you like it, I start to tease you now, spreading the oil with my fingers at the top of your thighs, along the crease where your bum cheeks start and sliding back and forwards along the inside of your open thighs only millimetres away from your hot open pussy.

Then finally I spread the oil on your bum cheeks. You feel some running down between them and you gasp as I pull your cheeks apart and watch as the oil dribbles down and gathers in your tight puckered little entrance. I blow on you there, knowing that you would love me to touch you or lick you there, but knowing if I did that I wouldn't get a chance to complete my massage … so I tell you to roll over. You tell me that I'm a terrible tease but you do it anyway, being much more wanton now … lying with your bum on the pillows, your legs wide apart and your arms stretched above your head.

I show you the tub of oil I am using. Coconut oil is solid at room temperature so as I scoop it out with my fingers it looks like the inside of a Bounty bar. I place a dollop of it on each or your nipples and tell you to watch. As it starts to react to your body heat, it starts to melt, turning to clear oil … little rivers running down from your hard nipples. "It tastes good too," I tell you, and to prove it I start to lick your left nipple before fastening my mouth over it … licking, sucking and gently nibbling as you run your fingers through my hair. My fingers are massaging your breasts, rubbing in the oil as I feel your nipple hardening in my mouth.

You let out a little groan as I take my mouth away so I can lean down and pick something up off the floor. It's a mirror … a magnifying mirror to be precise. I hold it at an angle so you can see, and place some of the semi-solid oil just above your clitoris. The way you are laying on the pillows means that your pussy is open and swollen, and we can both watch as the oil starts to melt and run down you onto your clit and then further down between your lips into your already wet pussy …

As I hold the mirror, I use my other hand to circle your clit as you watch … teasing it and you by not quite touching it, then finally rubbing my finger over it in the slippery oil, gripping it gently between my finger and thumb and squeezing it gently. As you continue watching in the mirror, I use two fingers to hold your lips wide apart so we can both see the oil mixing with your own juices inside you. Then, I slide two fingers just inside you, pressing them upwards against the front wall of your pussy and making your clit move by pressing the base of it from inside. I put the mirror down and lower my head to you, licking your clit before taking it into my mouth as

186

I had done with your nipple ... sucking it and nibbling on it as your pussy grips then releases my fingers inside you ... your fingers are in my hair ... guiding my mouth as you move your hips in a circular motion, using my mouth to give you pleasure. But then suddenly you pull my hair hard, making my body twist, the sudden change of balance forcing me onto my back as you climb on top of me.

You squat above my head facing my feet ... the combination of the oil and your juices dripping onto my face, and as I look through under your wide open thighs I watch as you fingers curl round my cock. You take some coconut oil and put it on the head of my cock, watching the white blob as it melts. Then you pull the skin back, spreading the oil all over the purple head before closing your mouth over it. The feeling of your lips, teeth and tongue are incredible, but then you put your hand into the ice bucket and bring it out dripping with icy water and you grab the base of my cock with your freezing fingers as your hot mouth sucks and licks the head .... and that's the last I see as you start to grind your pussy on my face, sliding back and forwards on my mouth and nose ... my tongue probing both pussy and bum hole as you slip and slide over me, a gasp coming from you every time your clit presses on my nose.

Then just as suddenly you stop, turn around and are kneeling over my cock. You tease me for a few seconds by rubbing your clit against the glistening head of my cock, but quickly lower yourself onto me, your lips parting then closing round me before you start to ride me hard. You grip my wrists and use me as support as you lean back, arching your body as my cock slides in and out of you ... your hips rotating as you do so that I am really screwing you ... or more accurately, you are screwing me. Then I feel you grip me inside. You are biting your lip, starting to cum. I thrust up into you … pushing hard … lifting us off the bed and finally we cum … my cock spurting up into your pussy as it pulses with your own climax … my cock bathed in your hot juice, oil and cum.

You collapse on top of me, your thighs round mine and we lay for a while getting our breath back. This progresses as we start to gently kiss and caress each other, fingertips lightly searching, teasing and probing. After a few minutes you start to work your way down my body with your mouth and finally I feel you take me into your mouth. As you suck my soft swollen cock, tasting both our cum, you slowly feel it swell and harden in your mouth. You pull the skin back and gently wank me and our eyes meet as you watch me watching your tongue and lips bring me back to life. You take your mouth away, your lips coated in my cum and you smile up at me before saying "I want you in my bum … now!"

I tell you to turn round and you kneel with your knees wide apart, your breasts and face pressed into the bed making your body one long curve up from your shoulders to your bum cheeks, rotating your hips out towards me … waiting.

Your bum cheeks are already parted enough for me to see the tight puckered entrance, but I use my hands to pull your cheeks wider, exposing you completely. You shudder as you feel me put a large lump of the coconut oil in my finger and rub it found and round your bum hole and then scrape my fingernail gently round and round your tight entrance, but the shudder turns into a long soft groan as you feel my tongue take the place of my finger and I lick round and round the tight dark opening.

You feel the pressure from my tongue increase as it starts to press inside you. You tighten and relax your muscles, trying to get my probing tongue in deeper, and finally you feel it slip inside, moving slowly inside you. You moan as you feel my tongue explore your bum but then you whisper, "Now! … Fuck me there NOW!!"

I pull back, then you feel my hard thick cock sliding between your pussy lips … you are just about to tell me that its not there that you want it when you realise that I am just getting my cock head covered in your juice to help it slip inside you. Using one hand still to hold your cheeks wide, I guide my cock into you with my other, pressing the head against your tight ring, sensing your body contractions as your muscles relax again and then pushing the whole head inside your bum.

You are so very tight … I don't move for a few seconds, and then I grip your hips. Rocking you slightly so that my cock starts slow fucking movements as you move back and forwards on me. You start to move on your own now, each rock getting slightly bigger, allowing you to take me in at your own speed … inch by inch … until suddenly you push back so hard I am right up inside you … "Fuck me hard now!" you shout, and I don't need telling twice, running my hand up your back to grab your hair, using it to control your movements as I fuck you harder and faster. My other hand slides under you to find your nipples, squeezing, pinching and stretching them as you push back against my every stroke.

Then I slide my hand down from your breasts, finding your clitoris and dripping pussy. Three fingers sliding in so easily as I finger-fuck you while ramming my cock hard into your bum. My thumb rubbing hard on your clit, I feel you start to cum again, and as your muscles tighten round me I can't stop either, my cock jerking and pumping in your tight ass as your pussy grips my fingers … floods of your juice running down over my hand …

I pull out … your bum hole gaping for a few seconds and I can see my cum lying inside you as your body shakes. I lie down on the bed and tell you to kneel above my face, and as you do I watch as you slide your finger into your bumhole, bringing it out covered in my cum. You start to suck your finger just as you feel my tongue entering you again … to clean you out.

# Also from Xcite Books

**20 bottom-tingling stories to make your buttocks blush!**
Miranda Forbes has chosen only the finest and sauciest tales
in compiling this sumptuous book of naughty treats!
Spanking has never been so popular. Find out why …

ISBN 9781906125837 price £7.99

# Tease Me

TEASE ME
20 Erotic Stories
Edited by Miranda Forbes

An exciting collection of erotic stories with mixed themes
that are certain to please and tease!

ISBN 9781906125844 price £7.99

# NEW! XCITE DATING

Xcite Dating is an online dating and friend-finder service. With Xcite Dating you can meet new friends, find romance and seek out that special person who shares your fantasies.

Xcite dating is a safe and completely anonymous service. Sign-up today – life's too short not to!

**www.xcitedating.com**

For more information about Xcite Books
please visit

**www.xcitebooks.com**

Thank you!